# COSPLAY

## The Comic-Con Killer

### ERNIE LEE

# OTHER WORKS BY ERNIE LEE

## NOVELS

**AQUASAURUS**, Aim-Hi Publishing, Canyon Lake, Texas
ISBN; 978-0-9971284-0-6, Trade paperback, 2016
ISBN; 978-0-9971284-2-0, Mass-market paperback,
ISBN; 978-0-9971284-1-3, E-PUB, 2016
ISBN; 978-0-9971284-9-9, Hardcover

**HIM**, Aim-Hi Publishing, Canyon Lake, Texas
ISBN; 978-0-9971284-4-4, Trade paperback, 2017
ISBN; 978-0-9971284-5-1, Mass-market paperback, 2017
ISBN; 978-0-9971284-7-5, E-PUB, 2017
ISBN; 978-0-9971284-9-9, Hardcover, 2017

**Search for Aquasaurus**
ISBN; 978-0-7321131-2-1, Trade paperback, 2017
ISBN; 978-0-7321131-1-4, Mass-market paperback,
ISBN; 978-0-7321131-3-8, Hardcover, 2017

## POETRY

**Where the Wild Rice Grows**, Aim-Hi Publishing Canyon
Lake, Texas 2017
ISBN: 978-0-9971284-3-7, Mass-market paperback 2017

Available:

WWW.Aim-HiBooks.com

# COSPLAY

## The Comic-Con Killer

# ERNIE LEE

Aim-Hi Publishing, LLC
1542 Lakeside Dr. W.
Canyon Lake, Tx 78133

Aim-Hi Publishing
1542 Lakeside Dr. West
Canyon Lake, Texas 78133
Publisher's Catalog-in-Publication Data
Names: Lee, Ernest (Ernie), 1946 - ;
  cover illustration:  Milan Javanovic __________
Title: COSPLAY; The Comic-Con Killer  / by Ernie Lee
Description: Aim-Hi Publishing LLC, 2021. | Summary: A serial killer continues to attack the same cosplay character at each Comic-Con. A rookie detective solves the case and tracks him down
Identifiers:
Library of Congress Control Number: 2021923686

ISBN **978-1-7321151-6-9** (Trade Paperback)
Subjects: Mystery – Fiction. | Serial killers – Fiction. | Comic-Con – Fiction. | Cosplay–
Fantasy – Superheroes – Comic books – Fiction.
**First Printing: November 2021**

Dedicated in loving memory of my mother, who loved a good story, who encouraged me to write, who loved to laugh, and who taught me to be thankful for each day as a gift from God.

# BETTY PAULINE WILLIAMS HENSON LEE HOUSEMAN CLOUD

## *Acknowledgements:*

There is much more to writing a book than a good story and putting sentences and paragraphs down on paper. This book is the product of several people who helped me put it together in a readable form. I would especially like to thank the following:

**Sandra Gayle Young,** who edited most of the chapters

**Billy James Wall** who encouraged me to finish this story.

**Liberty Fredericks**, who proofed and gave valuable feedback on middle drafts.

**Bob Eccleston**, who edited the final version.

**Lydia Luza Mousner** who provided valuable input and observations

Without your help, support, and assistance, I could not have completed this book. My heartfelt thanks go to each of you.

# COSPLAY

## 1

"Well, I don't like it, and I don't want her!"

Detective Sergeant Thornton Nix had just pushed his Captain's last button. Captain George Rangell rose to his full six-foot 7-inch frame over the seated Sergeant. His red face twisted into a ball of rage as he slammed his fist down hard on his desktop. The sound reverberated off the walls of his office. Unimpressed, Nix wondered if Rangell had broken his hand.

"I don't give a good hot damn what you like or what you want!" Rangell screamed.

"Yes, Captain."

"Damn it! Now, look at what you made me do! You made me cuss, and I promised Bunny I wouldn't do that anymore! Now we're going to have to have a 'go-to-Jesus' meeting tonight when I get home! Damn it!"

Rangell backhanded his yellow plastic pencil cup and sent it careening into the wall and bouncing into his round, battleship gray wastebasket. Pencils bounced and rolled across the floor.

"Shit!"

"Sorry, Captain."

"Don't give me that 'Captain' crap! We go back way too far, Thorn. I know who you are, and you know me. Chief's all up in this – way up in this. He's determined it's going to work, and we're the ones who's going to make it work! That's all there is to it!"

"Why?"

Rangell slumped back into his armchair and looked across the desk at a dejected Thorn Nix. The captain looked like a bulldog with his jaw set.

"Why? Because she just passed the detective examination with two years on the force. Nobody – **nobody** – has ever done that before. Not even you! That's why!"

"Why *me*?"

"Because you're the best cop I've got. This girl has a brain on her, Thorn. You can mold her into a good cop. She's smart. She'll learn fast."

"I'll retire first!" Thorn stared defiantly at his red-faced Captain.

"No, you won't," Rangell assured him as he tilted his chair back and displayed a self-satisfied smile. He had predicted this, and he had an ace in the hole. "You can't. Rule of 70."

"Rule of 70?"

"Yeah, remember that?" Rangell laughed. "The civil service rules say your age plus your years of service have to equal 70 before you are eligible to retire. You're 49 years old with twenty years of service. Add it up – that's only 69. You've got another year to go before you can even think about retiring!"

"But, George…"

"Don't "George" me! I can't get you out of this. Chief wants this to happen, or we're both on the hook!"

"What if I quit?" Nix threatened.

Rangell called his bluff with a chuckle. "You won't quit. You gonna walk out on your pension with a year left to serve? I don't think so." Rangell knew he had won. He smiled and gave Nix his "what ya gonna do?" face.

"But George, look at her. She looks like a damned Barbie doll in a cop outfit! If you look at her crosswise, she'll crack."

"She won't crack. She's been on patrol for two years," George assured him. "Them old boys out there have put her through the wringer. She won't crack. Everything that can be done to her has already been done – and then some. Besides, she won't be in uniform – plain clothes."

"And that name! Selma Cibolo! Whoever heard of a name like that? Selma **and** Cibolo. That's two suburbs on the northeast side!"

"The Cibolo name goes a long way back, Thorn. Her folks were among the Old 300, the first settlers Austin brought into this country when it was still Mexico. I heard her great granddaddy fought at the Alamo."

"Bullshit! There wasn't no Cibolo at the Alamo."

"It don't matter! She's a detective now, and she's assigned to you. And, you are going to make sure she's successful. Like it or not!"

"Well, I don't like it," Thorn asserted.

Captain Rangell rose from his chair again and walked to his window overlooking the parking lot along Market Street. He was trying hard not to curse again. He rubbed the palm of his hand against his mouth. "You don't have to like it, Thorn," he said calmly. "You just have to do it. It's a different world now. Things are changing, and we'd better change with it if we want to keep up."

"And I have to walk on eggshells? I've got to worry that every time something goes wrong, she'll be up here putting a bug in your ear?"

"I got your back. Ain't I always had your back, Thorn?"

"Yeah, but ..."

"No buts. All you got to do is make sure her beef don't get up to the Chief. I'll handle everything here. She's a trooper. She'll follow the chain of command – she probably knows it by heart." Rangell turned to face Nix again. He wanted Nix to see the sincerity in his eyes. "It won't get past me, so long as you don't step out of line."

"Step out of line?" Thorn asked.

"Yeah, as long as you are 'by the book.'" If you screw this up, Thorn, I'll have you in sensitivity training every week for the next year! You'll be so politically correct it'll be coming out your ears!"

"Crap!" Thorn groused.

"That, too." Rangell turned back from the window. "Now I've got to go home and tell Bunny what you made me say. Damn it!"

"Just lie to her," Thorn suggested.

"Lie to her? Lie to her? You lie to her and let me know how that works out for you, Hoss – the woman's a human lie detector. Shit!"

"That's it. Get it all out, now that you broke the ice!"

"Shut up and get out!"

Rangell felt himself getting angry again, but it was too late. Thorn had already cleared the door. A weary Captain George Rangell stooped over and fished his yellow pencil cup from his gray government trashcan.

# 2

A shadow moved as soft dawn light filtered around the drawn blinds into the darkened bedroom. It was quiet – not even a dog barked. Only the trash pickup ever marred the quiet seclusion in this neighborhood of lake homes, except for holidays or summer weekends. Jack picked this house for the isolation it offered – no noisy neighbors around to ask questions.

Jack squatted on his heels atop a maple dresser and watched the growing light filter into the room. Soon, it would be light enough to see the darkened heap lying on the bed. Jack knew what was lying there. He put her there. Now, she lay unmoving, not even breathing. She was his now, and nothing could change that. No one could interfere. No one could save her. He was free to use her as he pleased.

Jack leaped perch onto a nearby table and crouched like a vulture waiting for a feast. An expert at leaping, Spring-heeled Jack could jump incredible distances. He could vault tall buildings in a single bound. No one had ever caught him, though many tried. No one could capture Spring-heeled Jack. No one could find him. He felt safe because no one even knew who he was. They thought Spring-heeled Jack lived 150 years ago in England, far away from southern California. They were too stupid to understand.

The room gradually became brighter as the grey dawning increased. Objects began to become visible in the darkness. A collection of whips, belts, cat-o'-nine-tails, switches, rods, crops, and lashes lined the wall above the bed. Jack had sorted them by length and hung them neatly. The longer ones were on the outer ends, leading to the shorter items in the middle. The artistic arrangements formed an arc along the bedroom wall. Each day, Jack would take them down to clean, dust, and rehang them, precisely two measured inches from each other.

Nearby, the silhouette of Batman began to materialize in the growing dawn. Jack could barely make out Batman's hooded head against the pale window blinds. Soft neoprene draped Batman's shoulders and surrounded the upper part of his chest. The hood stretched down his face and ended at the bridge of his nose. The cheap imitations Jack had seen were crude by comparison. The sissies who wore cheap cloth hoods could never hope to be the real Batman. Only a custom-made neoprene fabric from Japan kept its shape and did not fade. The costume was impressive even in the fathomless, relentless black. Heavy satin was the thing for the long, flowing cape that fell to Batman's ankles. The blue form-fitting nylon suit was rippling over the physique of a real superhero. The sissies and freaks used foam muscles or artificial inserts. They could never hope to fill this suit with ridged power as Jack could. Jack needed no artificial foam muscles or synthetic six-pack abs to become Batman. However, today was not Batman's day. Today, Batman would be a silent witness to what was to come.

Another figure began to materialize in the growing light. Jack could make out the form of a nude manikin standing silently against the bare wall. The alabaster paleness of the plastic human-like figure showed that it was a male form. Unclothed, it seemed harmless and pathetic. Yet, it would stand as an impotent witness this fine morning. Later, when it was over, it would stand proudly against the wall, fully clothed in the light of day. Once Jack was sated in revenge, it would once again be dressed as Spring-heeled Jack.

It was light enough now to see the third witness, the one who loved her best. Jacob Frye. He stood, unspeaking with his top hat and cane, powerless to stop the coming violent revenge. Jack knew Jacob's cane concealed a blade; nevertheless, Jacob Frye stood frozen in his fear. He would stand and watch his sister's execution without blinking an eye. "Sister!" Jack shouted at the mute manikin. "Some sister!" She was his sister and his lover in a sick, perverted relationship they hid from the world. The upturned collar of Jacob's heavy leather jacket concealed the length of hair. Heavy leather gloves teeming with steel studs covered his arms. Like his sister, a sharp dagger protruded beneath his left wrist. It was with this blade that he carried out his vulgar assassinations. But not this day. Jack sprang from the table onto the floor and went to the figure of Jacob Frye.

"Not so buggery now, are you, mate?" Jack mocked the inert form. Jacob's vacant eyes stared toward nothing.

Jack removed his right glove and ran his bare finger down the blade extending from Jacob's wrist. The harmless plastic covering prevented a cut, but Jack knew the secret. He had designed it himself. A press against the hidden latch and the plastic sheath slid from the razor-sharp blade. Jack pressed the button, exposing the edge with a satisfying "zing." Jack ran his thumb down the knife with a smirk, drawing blood that dripped into his cupped palm. He showed his bloody hand to the lifeless statue.

"That's the only blood you will draw from me today, you weak, pathetic bastard," Jack snarled into the unseeing motionless face. "Too bad for you that I can't say the same about me." Jack's hysterical laughter filled the room.

Jack rubbed his thumb across the firm line of the doll's lips, painting them red with blood. "Now," thought Jack, "you look the perfect sissy."

Jack slowly turned toward the body on the bed. In the near dawn, he could faintly see her now. Evie Frye was bound and helpless. Dressed in midnight black like her brother and Batman, she lay flat on the bed with no pillow. Her heavy cloak was open on both sides of her shapely body and spread across the bed. Her bodice was unlaced and loosely laid across her chest to reveal soft, deep cleavage. A white sheet covered her nude lower body.

Jack turned back toward the helpless Jacob. "Nice, huh?" Jack motioned toward the figure on the bed. "She is ready and waiting. Can't you see her? Can you see how easy she is? You poor, worthless sod. Now the assassin becomes the victim, all for your viewing pleasure. First, look there! See the body of your sister-lover: Evie Frye, opened and waiting for her new lover? See how wanton she is? Watch her eyes as I take her from you! Then, watch as I take her from you forever!"

Jack gazed down at the doll on the bed and tried to imagine her alive. The unblinking form lay before him; her perfumed black hair lay in soft ringlets across her shoulders. Jack opened her bodice to reveal the satin chemise below. Spring-heeled Jack stood and slowly removed his clothing. Removing each article of clothing, he carefully placed it on the nude form until the manikin was once again fully costumed as Spring-heeled Jack.

There was another form nearby. It was a tall, dark, evil-looking form of a man. He wore a bloody apron and held a large meat-cutting knife, also stained with blood. He also wore a silk top hat and a black, heavy cloak. His mustached face was hard and unkind. He had dark, piercing eyes. He was not someone you would wish to meet in an alley. Just ask Mary Kelly, his final victim. Yes, it was the form of Jack the Ripper, Spring-heeled Jack's son.

Kneeling naked before Jack the Ripper, the nude Spring-heeled Jack bowed his head and begged for the honor.

"My son, how thrilled I am to be able to excise revenge from the evil bitch, Evie Frye. As your father, it is an honor as well as my duty. Look! Her brother watches nearby, with fear on his frozen face – paralyzed by fear. He is impotent. He is weak and can do nothing to save his shameless sister, Evie Frye, the most shameless and wanton assassin in the world! Neither she nor her impotent brother could kill you in open combat. Like cowardly hyenas, they ambushed you by night. Trapped and cornered, they eliminated you in a cruel, bloody butchery. She used her womanly charms to lure you to your death. She kissed you with passion, then covered your mouth with hers as she slid her blade deep into your heart."

"Then, they celebrated. Oh! How they celebrated your demise. Wrapped in the warm bloody arms of his sister, Jacob Frye received the pleasure you deserved. But you, you were Jack the Ripper! Little did they know that I – I endowed you with the ability to leap. Your ability is unconfined to distance or physical height. I taught you that. They did not know that you can leap to other worlds and void the dimension of time."

"My son, endow me now with your power. You grew much stronger than I. Now, I shall take the pleasure you were promised and denied. She will pay for what they did to you."

Satisfied, he rose and stood before Jack the Ripper. "Watch now as I make things right. Watch as I bring you back to life with the revenge you so richly deserve."

Turning toward the bed, he lay next to his unmoving victim. He took his knife and ran the blade down Evie's body, stopping at the top of the sheet. "There would be plenty of time for that later," he thought. He traced the knife across the naked abdomen above where the sheet lay. Running the blade across to the other side of her body, he trailed it across her ribs. He lowered his head and kissed her bare shoulder. Kneeling astride her, he placed the stiletto in the space between her breasts. He gripped and squeezed her through the gown. He looked at Jacob with a sneer.

"See how willing she is?" Jack mocked.

Jack leaned forward and ran his tongue down the places where his knife had been. When he reached the top edge of the sheet, he stopped and crossed to the other side. Then his tongue traveled back up, stopping short of her shoulder. He reached for the neck of her satin undershirt, and with a mighty yank, ripped it from her chest. Her jiggling breasts were exposed. With one last look at her brother, Jack closed his lips over her.

Jack sat upright in the bed and looked for the fear in the eyes of the doll beneath him.

"No!" he shouted. "It's not the same. It won't do at all! Damn it all! She's not real!"

With a shriek, he kicked the human-like doll off the bed. It landed in a heap in the corner at the feet of Jack the Ripper. Jack placed his face in his hands and cried. "She's not real!"

He wept until he fell asleep.

# 3

The telephone on Detective Thornton Nix's desk rang three times. Monday morning was always busy. When the phone rang, Thorn was across the room at the copier. He shot a look at his new partner, Selma Cibolo, who sat with her nose buried in a file folder.

*Ring.*

"You going to answer that?" he growled at her.

"Who? Me? Hell to the no! You told me two days ago never to answer your phone again -- ever!"

*Ring.*

Thorn could feel hackles rise between his shoulder blades. He narrowed his eyes as he struggled to contain his rising anger.

*Ring.*

For a moment, he considered writing her up for insubordination. The problem was that she was right. He had told her that.

"You'll answer it if I tell you to," he snarled.

"You didn't tell me to," she responded smugly.

*Ring.*

Glaring at Selma, Thorn grabbed his copies from the machine. With thudding, giant steps, he stomped back to his desk, where he snatched up the receiver. The hard plastic handset smacked sharply into his left ear.

"Homicide! Thorn here!"

While Thorn talked into the phone, Selma allowed herself a satisfied smile – not one that Thorn would notice, but one that gave her a lot of personal pleasure. Pretending to read the file, Selma listened to the conversation.

"Where? When? How long has she been there? On the way! Right!" he barked, only pausing a few seconds between scribbling notes. He slammed the handset down so hard it bounced off the cradle and rolled across the desk onto the floor. Selma had to fight to keep from laughing, and she struggled to keep the smile off her face. Too late, she could tell Thorn saw it.

He scowled at Selma, trying to control himself as he fished the instrument back up on the desk by its cord. He gently placed it on the cradle. If she were a man, Thorn would have thrown the phone at her. It was a different world now, the Captain had said. Things were changing, and we had better change with it if we wanted to keep up. He knew the Captain was right.

Don't mess this up – or else! Thorn had already spent three days in hell at a sensitivity class. He did not want to go back. Detective Selma Cibolo sat reading her cold case file. There was no doubt she was smart. Two years of patrol, and she almost aced the detective examination. The Captain made it clear it was Thorn's job to make it work. But there was no way the Captain could have known how stubborn this woman was. Thorn took a deep breath and walked slowly over to Selma's desk. He ran his hands across the top edge of the chair before he sat in it.

"Look," he began. "You waltzed in here two days ago like you owned the place. I didn't see any deference or respect out of you. You grabbed up my phone like *you* were the lead detective and not me. You didn't have a clue what you were doing. So, I told you not to answer my phone. What I meant was not to answer it on your own – I didn't mean, 'never!' You and I are going to have to work together for a long time, so let's get this settled once and for all." For some reason, Thorn felt like he was treading in deep water. It was hard to move against the current.

"Is there an apology in there somewhere?" she asked in an innocent voice.

"*Damn her! She knows exactly the position I'm in,*" Thorn thought. Thorn felt trapped. He cradled his head in his meaty hands and brushed his hair back.

"Yeah. Okay, I'm sorry. Like I said, we're going to be together for a long time, and we're going to say some things to each other that we'll probably both regret. We're going to be hot and tired and frustrated at everything that's going on. We've got to learn to get past all that noise and get on with the business at hand. Neither one of us wants to walk on eggshells all the time or be pissed off every day."

At that moment, Selma felt her respect for Thorn grow. For a man like him to apologize like that to a rookie must be humiliating. Selma nodded in agreement. Thorn rose from the chair and towered above her.

She looked up at him and smiled as she said, "Okay. You're right – I guess I was trying to impress you. I was eager to get off on the right foot, and I stepped on your toes. I get it."

"All right! I get carried away sometimes too. I'll work on it." He rose from the chair and walked toward the door. "We roll in five minutes. Get ready."

"Yes, sir." For the first time, he had treated her like a real person; and for the second time since she met him, she called him 'sir.' *"Maybe I do have a chip on my shoulder,"* Selma thought. She'd work on that too.

In the car, Thorn briefed her as he drove. Someone found a body in a dumpster behind the old Kiddie Park on Broadway. A construction crew discovered it and called the cops. The cops took one look and called Thorn.

The detectives moved through the dense San Antonio morning traffic without running lights or the siren. There was no need to run code; there rarely was for the homicide squad. Winding through Brackenridge Park, Thorn cruised to a stop behind the old amusement park on Brackenridge Way. He parked on a side street to keep from blocking traffic on Broadway. The dumpster was tucked into a small unfenced area along the road.

The owners billed Kiddie Park as the oldest children's amusement park in America. It was plush in its time, but now the place was a dump. The old wooden benches and rides were weatherworn and sagging. In the 1930s, the playground was probably a wonderland with a merry-go-round, bumper cars, and little boats floating on a circular algae-filled pond. It looked like the only thing the custodians had kept up was the merry-go-round. The paint was peeling off everything else, and weeds were thigh-high in the corner by the fence. The San Antonio Zoo Association had recently bought the park and intended to move it closer to the zoo down the street. This space on

Broadway was much too valuable to be occupied by a decrepit old kiddie park. It was a beautiful pecan grove setting in its day but had slowly slid into urban decay. The only occupants of the area now were winos and drug dealers. In a year, no one would remember it, just like the old and abandoned Play Land Park a few blocks north. People drive by those places now and never even realize it was there. Both parks deserve better than that. Thorn hoped the zoo people would take better care of it when they reopened.

A pair of police officers stood near a beat-up steel garbage dumpster. At the end of the street toward Broadway, five flashing police cars stood with their doors ajar.

Thorn and Selma got out of the car. "What's that all about?" Thorn pointed. "They with you?" he asked the pair of officers standing by the dumpster.

"Nah," the Sergeant shook his head. "Someone ran over some old bum last night and left him in the ditch. It's a separate call."

"Hi, Selma," the younger officer said.

"Hi, Bran," Selma nodded. "Good to see you again."

The patrol Sergeant looked at Selma and raised his eyebrows.

"This is my new partner," Thorn told him. "Selma Cibolo, have you met Sergeant Howe?"

"No, we've been on different squads," Selma said, "but I've heard of him. Good to meet you, Sergeant." She took his offered handshake, which he held just a fraction too long. Selma sighed and stepped back.

"Selma, how about going down to the corner?" Thorn pointed toward a place across Broadway. "Get us a couple of coffees; why doncha?"

"One of them for me?" Selma blurted out without thinking, regretting the cynicism in her voice.

Thorn clamped his jaw tight as he handed her a fiver. "Get four, okay?" he said pointedly. *"Didn't this girl know that in Texas, a couple was a nonspecific number less than five? More than five were a few. Who knew how many a bunch was? Screw it! She needs to lighten up,"* he thought before turning his attention back to the Sergeant.

"I'll go with you," Officer Bran Stevens offered. "Help you carry it back."

"How's it goin'?" Bran asked as soon as they were out of earshot.

"Good," Selma answered, although she didn't mean it. She and Bran were partners on traffic patrol last year. He knew her better than that.

"It doesn't look so good," Bran grinned. "He been riding you some?"

"Is it that obvious?" Selma asked.

"He's just old school," Bran assured her. "It's part of the job. To him, you're a rookie again. It'll get better. Once he trusts you, it'll get better. You have to learn to mask it, that's all. Quit letting it get to you. Stop letting him see it. If you don't," Bran paused, "you ain't gonna make it."

"I know, Bran. But, man! He gets under my skin."

"Yeah, he can do that," Bran laughed. "Persevere, my dear – persevere." Bran nudged her arm with his elbow reminding her of their class motto during the academy. Persevere.

By now, they had drawn alongside the disturbance at the end of the one-lane street. Selma knew most of the officers gathered around a private ambulance. A bearded man lay under a sheet on the elevated stretcher. The medics had wound a bandage around his head.

"He just whooped past like nobody's business and clipped me with the side of his ambulance. Damn fool ought to be fired," the old man wailed.

"Which ambulance service was it?" A cop with a clipboard asked.

"Hell! I don't know. Don't you know who your ambulance is?" The old man was cranky and combative. He was probably in some pain. "I woke up this mornin' with a splittin' headache and a knot on my head."

The cops acknowledged Selma and Bran as they passed. When they returned with the coffee, the ambulance, the old man, and cop cars were all gone.

Back at the dumpsters, Sergeant Howe and Thorn had their heads inside a large blue trash bin. The coroner arrived as they walked up, so Selma passed him her coffee. She didn't want it anyway; it was the principle of the thing. The little group made room as the coroner set up a ladder and climbed into the dumpster. It was a laborious effort. A photographer moved from side to side to get different angles as the coroner did his job. A couple of ambulance attendants stood by, ready to retrieve the body when the coroner gave his okay.

After a while, the assistants helped the coroner climb out of the steel box. It took even longer for him to get out. The coroner, Dr. James, cleaned his hands and raised his coffee cup in salute to Selma, thanking her for the coffee. They watched as the attendants hoisted the limp body out of the dumpster and carried it to a waiting gurney. Selma saw the victim for the first time.

The body wore a long, sweeping skirt of reddish maroon under a black studded leather tunic. A studded black leather belt circled the waist. The skirt tucked into the belt partway around, leaving a wide expanse of thigh showing. Knee-high plastic boots overlapped remnants of black tights that had been cut or torn away above her boot tops. A fake plastic dagger hung from a belt on her hip, and black leather gloves rose to her elbows. A bayonet-like rubber knife extended past the palm under her left wrist, but the right glove had none. Long black hair hung down past a large turned-up vampire collar.

"Evie Frye," Selma spoke aloud without intending. "It's Evie Frye!"

She had Thorn's immediate attention. "You know this girl?"

"No," Selma shook her head. "No, I – I don't know her, but she's dressed like Evie Frye."

"Who is Evie Frye?" Thorn demanded.

"She's … well, … she's an assassin," Selma confessed.

"An assassin?" Thorn asked, his eyes wide with excitement.

"This girl's name is Evie Frye?" the coroner asked, writing it down on his pad.

"No … wait!" Selma pleaded. "No. The body's name is not Evie Frye – I don't know who *she* is."

"Who the hell is Evie Frye?" Thorn repeated, losing his patience again. Taking Selma's arm, he guided her away from the group to the other side of their patrol car. He did not want the others to hear.

"Evie Frye is a fictional character," Selma began, "an assassin from a video game – Assassin's Revenge. The girl is dressed like her – **not** her.

"Why in the world would a girl go around dressed like an assassin from a video game?"

"Comic-Con was in town," Selma said.

Thorn grimaced as if he had a headache. "Comic-Con," he grumbled. "You mean those freaks that go around dressed up like it's Halloween, even in the summer?"

"It's a comic convention – Comic-Con. The kids – even adults sometimes come dressed as their favorite characters. This one is dressed up like Evie Frye. It's called cosplay. Don't you see what this means?" Selma asked.

"She was a nut case?" Thorn offered.

"No," Selma said. "It means she attended Comic-Con yesterday. It's a clue -- we can find out more about her there. They may even have a video." A commotion behind them distracted Thorn's attention.

"Forget it; we've got a real person dead over there. Let's concentrate on solving her murder; why don't we? Go check out the body before they take it away and see if you can get some real clues. Not comic book ones," he added as he returned to the dumpster.

The assistants were fishing something out of the dumpster, which the police examined. It appeared to be a dirty rag.

"Whewww," one cop muttered. "Hey, Doc! Come check this out."

Selma pulled the sheet from the victim's head. Pretty girl. About 18 or so. No holes in her face other than earrings. No visible tats. Selma continued her examination as she pulled the sheet down. She lifted the girl's arm and removed the left glove. She wasn't married.

"Chloroform?" Thorn asked.

Dr. James waved his hand over the rag to get the scent and shook his head.

"No, that's not chloroform. It's probably some sort of cleaning solvent. What else did you find in there?" He asked the assistants, still rummaging around in the dumpster.

"Just some old mops, a bunch of rags, and some empty bottles, pieces of wood …" the searchers replied.

"Let me see those bottles," the coroner requested.

Two plastic gallon jugs came flying out of the dumpster at Thorn's feet. He picked one up, unscrewed the cap, and passed it over to Dr. James.

The coroner nodded his head and read the label. "Surface cleaner – that's not what killed her," he decided. "Custodial staff probably dumped this stuff Saturday before the body got here."

"What do you think, Doc?" Thorn asked. "Any idea what killed her then?"

Dr. James shook his head, "She's got rope burns around her wrists and neck. She was probably asphyxiated or strangled, more than likely raped. Of course, we won't know until we run some tests and examine the body more carefully. I don't think this was an overdose. I didn't see any gunshot or stab wounds. There was no blood at all except in the striations around her neck. It may have been some sex play, and they probably panicked when she stopped breathing. I think they threw her in the dumpster and ran away."

"You said 'they,' Doc. Does that mean you think there was more than one assailant?"

"Well," the doctor tilted his head, "it took two of us to get her out of the dumpster. It had to be a pretty big guy to put her in there by himself."

The attendants laughed with each other and repeated "us" as they loaded the body into the waiting ambulance as the coroner got into his car. When they were gone, Thorn signed the police officers' reports and released them from the scene.

Thorn and Selma were alone at the murder scene. Thorn picked up the rags and empty plastic bottles and threw them back inside the bins.

"Thorn," Selma began, "why don't we check the Comic-Con organizers and see what we can find out?"

"Selma," Thorn's voice tensed, "when we get back, why don't you get with dispatch and see what ambulance calls were over here last night? Maybe they saw something. That would be more helpful, don't you think?"

"No problem," she admitted, "but video from inside the Convention Center might show who she was hanging out with, don't you think?" she mimicked him. He noticed.

"Wouldn't he be in costume? Even if we saw someone with her, we wouldn't know who he was, or even if it was the right – what's her name? Elsie?"

"Evie. It might tell us …," Selma began.

"Look!" Thorn became authoritative. "We've got enough to check on. We're gonna stick with good police work. Identify the victim, interview the parents, and review the coroner's report. You know, *police work*. It's probably someone she knows or a boyfriend she went to the party with."

"I know, we'll do that too …."

Thorn interrupted again as he got in the car and slammed the door, "Selma, get in the car! I've got 15 open cases on my desk right now. Each one of them needs work. Let's get on *those* cases with *real* people. We don't have time to chase Batman down a rabbit hole!"

# 4

Selma looked at the two stacks of case files on her desk. There was one stack of open case files and another stack of cold cases. It would take weeks, if not months, to go through them all. If Thorn had ordered her not to follow up her Comic-Con lead, he could not have been more effective. Selma believed Thorn planned to swamp her with minor detail work; keep her busy so she would not have time to go off in a different direction. Control freak!

On top of that, new murder cases were happening almost daily. San Antonio was growing fast and becoming a dangerous place to live. From 2015 to 2016, homicides increased from 94 to 140. Now, 2017 was stacking up at a similar rate. Selma realized workload was one factor for her promotion. Thorn and Selma were only one of six teams working in the Homicide Division. The workload swamped every team in the division.

There was a daily stream of people coming into the homicide office for interviews. Witnesses, suspects, informants, and criminals of all sorts sat in or milled about the waiting room. Some came voluntarily, others – not so much. When one of them showed up, Thorn would make Selma stop her research and sit in the interview room while he interviewed them. Rarely allowed to speak or ask a question, Selma realized she was mainly there for dramatic effect and to take notes.

"Just sit there and look pretty," Thorn had told her. He had not even realized how condescending that comment was. It wasn't the first time she had heard it, and she realized it wouldn't be the last either. Anyway, she thought, at least I have a seat at the table, and that's something.

Selma was not opposed to paying her dues, but she wanted and needed to believe she was doing something significant. It shouldn't be like the scouts sending out a new camper to look for left-handed smoke sifters or go snipe hunting. Selma held her tongue and worked her way through a mountain of files and documents. Her time would come.

Before she could dive back into the stacks of cases, Thorn told her to go down to check with dispatch; then check missing person reports. It shouldn't be hard to identify the victim. Surely, someone would be looking for her. The girl didn't look like a runaway or a prostitute. Also, ambulances do not just run around willy-nilly. Someone has to dispatch them. A 911 call would go through dispatch, and there would be a record of the response. If it were a private ambulance, there would be a record too, but you had to find the hospital or ambulance company that made the call.

"Not Amie Frye, either!" Thorn barked as she left the room.

"Evie," Selma reminded over her shoulder.

"Whatever! I want her *real* name," he shouted as Selma disappeared down the hallway.

Selma rode the elevator down to the basement. Within five minutes, she determined that the murder victim was probably eighteen-year-old Hanna Gleason, a white female, missing since Sunday. Another team would notify the next of kin and arrange for them to identify the body.

Selma was glad she didn't have to do that part. It was horrible. Working the crime scene was bad enough.

Dispatch had no record of calls to that section of town Sunday night. The city required a fire unit to respond to all city ambulance and 911 calls. The only call to that area in the last 24-hours was the 9 a.m. call Selma had seen from the crime scene. A vehicle ran over a pedestrian and had fled the scene. That was the report she needed to find. There were no calls to that location on Sunday night.

It must have been a private ambulance company that made the call. There were several private emergency transportation companies; however, they were competitors and did not work well together. They roved the entire city and did not have designated territories. It was dog-eat-dog business out there. Selma figured the easiest way to identify which company made the call would be to call each one individually. Since there were more ambulance companies in the city than hospitals, Selma figured the easiest thing was to phone all hospitals first.

After three hours of phone work, Selma determined that no one checked into any emergency rooms by a private ambulance. There were several 911 deliveries but only a handful of POV deliveries. Dead end. The only thing left to do was call each ambulance company one at a time. Where would that hit-and-run ambulance have been going? Nursing home? Emergency care clinic? If it was an ambulance, why would they just drive off and leave the bum there? Maybe, they didn't know they hit him, Selma reasoned. There was only one way to find out, and it was going to take several more hours.

Selma created a new case file for Hanna Gleason and entered the notes on her laptop. The city recently transitioned to electronic records rather than bulky paper files. She e-mailed the Coroner and the photographer to add documents. She would receive a notification when the Coroner had filed his report. Thorn was pacing the room deep in thought. He was trying to make some sense of it and failing miserably.

"How could a girl with all that going for her end up in a dumpster?" he muttered aloud. "She should have been safe anywhere in town, especially the crowded Civic Center. How did she end up over on Broadway, five miles away? It makes no sense." He circled the desk a few more laps in silence before he came to a stop. He stood silently for a moment before speaking.

"Selma, if you can stop what you're doing, let's go find that wino." It wasn't a request.

Selma turned the job of contacting private ambulance companies over to an intern in central administration and joined Thorn in the car. Slowly cruising through Brackenridge Park, they kept their eyes peeled for their bum. They did not see their prey anywhere along the side streets or entries to the park. They drove up and down Broadway for twenty minutes before they saw a man lying on the benches at Joske Pavilion. They got out of the car and approached the man before he could run.

"Hey, man," Thorn spoke casually to the unshaven man, trying to put him at ease. "How are ya? You okay?"

The nervous man sat up and appeared ready to walk away. "Yeah, I'm okay – no problems, man. I'm just layin' here a minute. You the cops?"

"Yeah, but don't worry – it's all right. You're okay. We're just trying to find someone – that's all."

"What'd he do?"

"Nah! It's nothing like that, man. He didn't do anything. It's more like something was done to him, you know?"

"Somethin' like what?"

"Something like getting hit by a car."

"Man, I don't know nothin' 'bout that." The man put up his hands as if to push the idea away.

"We're just checking to make sure he's okay, you know? We can't find him, that's all."

"That's all you want?"

"That's all. But if you don't know him, we'll leave you be."

"Well, I don't know nothin', but I heard somethin'."

"What did you hear?"

"Feller named Papa Joe got hit over there last night, I heard." He pointed toward Kiddie Park. "Knocked 'em out, and he laid there all night 'til daylight came."

"Yeah, that's the guy. Pappa Joe, you say?"

"Yeah, that's how I know 'em – Papa Joe."

"Do you know where we can find Papa Joe? We want to make sure he's okay."

"No, I don't. I know where he hangs out, though – you might find 'em there. Check over to the Pig Stand. If he's there, he'll probably be under the bridge somewhere around back. Is he in trouble?"

"No way, man. We're trying to find out who hit him."

"Well, I hope you do. It's gettin' where you can't even walk down the road around here anymore without somebody tryin' to run you down."

"Well, we'll do what we can. Is there anything we can do for you? What's your name?"

"You can call me Stephen. You got any money?"

Thorn handed Stephen a couple of dollar bills and walked back to the unit with Selma. They drove into the parking lot at the Pig Stand but didn't see Papa Joe anywhere around.

"Well, this looks like a dead-end," Thorn declared as he headed back to the station.

Selma decided to take a chance. "What about me going over to the Civic Center and see what I can find? It might be a dead-end too, but we might get lucky."

Thorn gave her the look. "Man, you don't give up, do you?"

Selma smiled, "That's what you wanted for this job, wasn't it? Someone that doesn't give up."

Thorn smiled and had to admit she was right. He shook his head in surrender.

"Yeah. Sometimes you need to be a bird dog on this job. All right, drop me off at the station, and you can check them out on your way home tonight. No overtime!" He stressed.

Selma checked with security and found Mickey Garner staffing the desk. After flashing her badge, it didn't take long for Mickey to have the tapes in the viewer. They would have to look at them in real-time, so Selma expected to be there for hours. Mickey was going off shift. "Not to worry," he told her. The night person, Ray Thomas, could get her anything else she needed.

Selma watched the Saturday film for three hours, not noting anything unusual. It was a split-screen, so she got six views. She could expand each segment to full-screen if she needed a closer look. Vehicles and people came and went with regularity. At around five o'clock on the tape, a group of custodians emerged on the loading dock. Each one pushed a rolling wastebasket, and some drug a second one behind them. They dumped their loads into the bins and returned up the ramp.

Evening fell, and lights came on when the center closed. Selma scribbled some notes and asked Ray to load the Sunday tape. Selma was already past the end of her shift. Realizing she may not have another chance to check things out, Selma made a snap decision.

"Ray, do you have copies of these tapes I can take with me?"

"You bet! You want them?" he asked.

"Well, yeah! You got them?" Selma responded.

Ray handed her a packet of DVDs and said, "You won't be able to enlarge the screens, but if you see something you want, you can bring it back, and we'll blow it up for you.

"You made copies of the entire Comic-Con?" Selma asked.

"Yeah," Ray said sheepishly. "Some of the guys like to look at the costumes during slow times around here," he blushed. "Some of those costumes …" he trailed off.

"Yeah, I've seen them," Selma admitted. "Which cameras are on here?"

"All of 'em," Ray admitted.

"All of them? Including the dock?"

"Yep."

"I can take them with me?" Selma asked, not believing her luck.

"They're yours," Ray replied. "Do what you want with them. There's another set here."

What a break! Selma would not have to stay at the Civic Center all night reviewing Comic-Con tapes. She could go home and play them on her computer.

Alone in her bedroom, Selma watched Comic-Con deep into the night. By three in the morning local time on the Sunday tape, Selma found what she was looking for: Hanna entered dressed as Evie Frye. She was alone as she walked down the central aisle.

Copying down the tape times, Selma followed Hanna through the vast hall. There were only a few obstructed locations. In some places, high booth displays blocked some visibility. There were no cameras in the restrooms, and most of the backstage area was out of sight, but almost everywhere else was visible. For three hours, no one approached Hanna except occasionally to take her picture. Hannah did not buy anything from the booths except for a soft drink from the refreshment stand. She sat alone at a table in the refreshment area and sipped a soda.

There were several more hours of tape left. Sometime in the night, an exhausted Selma fell asleep watching her computer screen. She did not see a costumed group gather around Hannah. She did not see one of the characters lead Hannah out of the camera view. Selma did not see a white wheelchair van pull up to the loading dock or a man push a wheelchair into the building. She did not see a man load an unconscious woman into the truck and speed away.

When Selma awoke, sunlight streamed through her windows. She was already late to work. She would not get back to those videos for several months. By then, it would not matter.

# 5

"I saw her on the videos," Selma revealed to Thorn. "She didn't seem to be with anyone, but it looked like she was waiting for someone."

"A boyfriend?" Thor asked.

"It's possible," Selma admitted.

"Lots of things are possible; only a few things are significant," Thorn informed her. He sat for several moments, rubbing his chin as he thought. Finally, he shook his head.

"I'm thinking the boyfriend was late or didn't show, so someone else picked her up, and she left with the new guy."

Something did not add up for Selma. Thor's theory was possible, but Hannah didn't seem to be that type of girl.

"Either that," Thorn continued, "or the boyfriend shows up late, they have a big fight, and things got out of hand."

"How did he get her out of the civic center with thousands of people around?"

"Maybe they left together and went somewhere else – maybe Brackenridge Park – and things got violent. It happens."

"They were just kids," Selma reminded him.

"Some school kids out at Live Oak offed their schoolmate a few years back. It happens."

"I'll check a list of friends and see if I can find out who she was going to the show with."

"Did you find that ambulance driver yet?"

"No, I haven't finished contacting all the private companies. I'll get that list back from Anita in Central Admin and follow up."

Thorn shook his head, "No, go ahead and let Admin finish it. You call her friends and find out what they know. Don't spend a lot of time, but try to find out who she hung out with."

"What about other gamers who played Assassin's Revenge?"

Thorn frowned at her. "You're not going to give up that angle, are you?" Thorn asked, peeved.

"No, I haven't. There's a string there that we need to pull."

"Look. Don't make this more complicated than it has to be. She either met someone at the event or left with someone she knew. If you plan on going after some comic book character, you do it on your own after getting the facts. Call all those kids, but don't waste time on this game crap. I need facts, not fairy tales. I want *real* killers, not comic book superheroes. Got it?"

"Yeah, yeah, I got it." Selma hated Thor's domineering, know-it-all attitude. His was the final opinion, and it didn't matter to him whether Selma agreed or not. Selma closed her notebook and went to her desk to find out if anything had turned up on the ambulance companies.

The clerk assigned to the case, Anita, reported no results yet. Most of the private companies were reluctant to share information on their calls because of privacy laws. But so far, none of them reported a unit being around Brackenridge Park that night.

Over the next week, Selma updated Hannah's file with photos and lists of her friends and hobbies. The family did not even list cosplay as one of Hannah's pastimes. Selma worked her way through the list of Hannah's friends, calling each one briefly. About halfway down the list, Selma dialed a number for a boy named Gene Smith.

*Ring*

"S'up?" A young voice answered.

"Hello! Can I speak to Gene Smith, please?"

"Speaking. Who's this?"

He sounded like a normal young man. Selma told him who she was and what she wanted.

"Yeah, I knew her," Gene admitted. "She was a good friend. It is a shame what happened to her. She was the last person you'd think would end up like that," he added. He did not sound nervous – just sad. "Have you found out what happened yet?"

"Not yet, but we are trying. Maybe you can help us, Gene," Selma added hopefully.

"I'll try, but I wasn't with her at the time. I wasn't allowed to go to the Comic-Con that day – I couldn't meet her like I promised."

Selma sat up straight in her chair. "You were supposed to meet her there?"

"Yes, ma'am. We were supposed to meet in the snack bar after church Sunday, but I got in trouble and couldn't go. Mom took my phone, so I couldn't even call her to let her know I wasn't coming. I think maybe if I was there, it might not have happened."

"Gene, you can't think that way. It's not your fault. If you were there, it might have happened to both of you."

"That's what my mom said, too."

"Who else was supposed to meet her there?"

"It was just us, I think. Hannah might have mentioned it to some others, but I don't know."

"Can you give me a list of her closest friends that may have shown up?"

Selma scribbled down the names as quickly as Gene named them. There were not that many. Selma hesitated. Should she go down that road? Selma decided to take a left turn in the investigation,

"Gene, do you know the game 'Assassin's Revenge'?"

"Oh, yeah," he admitted. "It's not my favorite game, but I play it some."

"Do you know if Hannah ever played the game?"

"Oh, sure – she loved it. She would talk about it all the time, but I could never get that much into it. I have to study a lot to keep my grades up for the Honor Society.

That game takes a lot of time. I'm limited on how long I can play."

"What would Hannah say about the game?"

"She liked it. She played it all the time. She'd tell me about stuff that happened when she played. It was Hannah's favorite game. She played a lot more than I did."

"What is the game about?" Selma asked.

"It's mainly about a group of assassins – but these are good assassins."

"How can an assassin be good?" Selma asked, even though she already knew the answer.

"They only kill bad guys – guys like Jack the Ripper and stuff like that. They rid the world of killers, criminals, and those kinds of people. They never kill the good guys."

"So, how do you play?"

"You adopt a character – either a good assassin or one of the bad guys. There is a whole list of characters you can select. You have to pick one that's not being used at the time. Then the good ones try to track down the bad guys and kill them without getting killed themselves. It's interactive, so you've got to search through towns and buildings and caves and stuff. They move around a lot, so it's not easy to find them, but they leave clues. The bad guys are trying to escape to a place where you are powerless to harm them – or they attack and knock you out of the game. It's pretty intense and graphic."

"Who was your character?"

"I usually picked Jacob Frye," Gene admitted.

"Why did you pick him?" Selma asked.

Gene laughed. "I don't know. I guess because Hannah was usually Evie Frye. Jacob was her brother. I thought maybe - you know - I might get closer to Hannah, so I played as Jacob. They worked together. I thought if there were two of us, we'd be harder to knock out."

"Do you know who the other players were?"

"You can never tell. It's always different. You can look at the player profile, but it usually only gives a player name – not their real name. I only found out she played Evie Frye because she talked about it a couple of times. Every time you play, there might be a different person in those roles, depending on who's online at the time. You can set the game in friends mode, but then everyone has to play at the same time that way. That's hard to manage, especially with clubs and sports and stuff. So you sign on and play with whoever is online. The characters don't change, only the players behind them. Sometimes you would sign on and find that someone knocked you out of the game while you were gone. Then, you'd just reset and start the game again. You kept your points."

"Points?"

"Yeah," Gene replied, "you get points for playing the game. There are goals and battles—stuff like that. Before you quit, you need to go to a safe place before you log out. If you forget, your character is sort of left out there."

"So, if you looked at the profile of a player, you couldn't tell who it was in the real world?"

"No, you can't tell real names or anything. You can sometimes tell what state they live in, and their player name – stuff like that. You can text them from inside the game. If they don't tell you who they really are, you'd never know. But, it didn't matter much; the next time you play, it might be someone else anyway."

Selma would check with the game manufacturer to see if they archived those inside the game chats. "Did you ever play with Hannah?"

"Sure, lots of times. We'd text outside the game and meet inside the game. Most players were from out of state. It's a pretty big game, and you'd have to be playing at the same time. There's probably a million people playing at the same time."

"Let me ask you, Gene. If I wanted to know who was playing a character at any one time, how would I find out? Let's say I wanted to know Evie Frye's real identity. Would I be able to find out if I wanted to?"

"Only if she told you." Gene's voice fell to a whisper as he confided, "Sometimes it's not even a girl."

"How would you know you were playing with Hannah?"

"I knew her profile name. You could text her and ask if she was playing and where she was in the game. Or, you could text her from inside the game. That's about the only way. You could ask for a phone number, but no one ever gives that out. Lots of players won't even give you their e-mail. But they will ask you to like their social media page sometimes."

"Were you and Hannah friends on social media?"

"Sure, we were also both on our class page and other social media sites. But, she and I never chatted or messaged each other much. Comic-Con was going to be our first time getting together outside school."

"Do you have Hanna's e-mail address? Can I have it?"

"Sure," Gene admitted. After looking it up, Gene spelled it out for Selma.

"One more thing, Gene,"

"Yes, ma'am?"

Selma cringed at the "ma'am." She was not *that* old.

"What was Hanna's player name?"

Gene thought for a moment. "Uh … yeah! I remember. Her last name was Gleason, so it was her name. It was *HanGlee*."

Selma told Gene goodbye and rang off. Selma wrote notes in her notebook, including all the information Gene gave her. She wrapped the book with a thick red rubber band and laid it aside.

In the police file, she wrote, *"Telephone interview with Gene Smith, Classmate of V. Phone 555-275-8477. 17 years old. Knew V, but not a close friend. Provided e-mail address for V but little else. Player username: HanGlee. Players can text each other from within the game. No follow-up required for G.Smith – not a suspect."*

At that moment, Selma decided to make her own investigation into Hannah's death. Thorn said she could follow up cosplay leads on her own time. Thor would remember that when things got hot. Selma didn't know if Comic-Con had anything to do with Hannah's death or not, but she was determined to find out.

# 6

"Ewwwwe," Shiree Davis drew back in disgust, "that's gross. I'm not doing that!"

"Well, you said you wanted something different," Kendra laughed and teased her. "That's different!"

"Yeah -- too different!" Shiree agreed as she picked up another comic book and flipped through the pages. Her friend, Kendra, paged through the laptop, looking for characters.

"I'm going as Harley Quinn," Kendra stated. "I already have the outfit."

"You, and about 500 other people. I want a character no one else is going to use."

"Like who?" Kendra asked.

"I don't know; that's why I'm looking. What do you see on the laptop?"

"Just the regular costumes everyone else is wearing."

Shiree took the laptop. "Here, let's look at some game characters." After half an hour, the girls had not decided on a suitable costume. Shiree sighed and pushed the laptop away. "I'll guess I'll have to go as Wonder Woman, like a thousand other girls."

"Wait – who's this?" Kendra laughed. "Nice."

Shiree took the laptop. "Yeah, that's more like it. Who is she?"

"Someone named Evie Frye," Kendra said. "She's in a game called Assassin's Revenge."

"At least a lot of people will want your picture, but I bet I'll get more than you do. No one's going to know who you are," Kendra teased her friend.

"I'll bet a lot of people stop and ask me who I am," Shiree said. "I'll bet I get a lot more pictures than you do. Everyone has Harley Quinn."

Kendra gathered her sweater and purse as she brushed off her skirt. "I've got to go. Let me know what you decide, okay? Which day are you going?"

"I've got to go on Saturday. What day are you going?"

"I can't go Saturday – family stuff. I'll have to go Sunday."

"Can't they let you out of it? Denver Comic-Con only comes around once a year."

"No, probably not; it's a family reunion. I don't think they'll let me go, but I'll ask. Maybe they'll let me go in the afternoon."

"That's perfect! I can't get down there until noon anyway. We can meet and go together."

"Don't count on that! I may not get to go at all. We'll just plan to meet there, and if I don't show up, at least you'll be there already."

"Text me and let me know, okay?"

"Yeah, and you text me and tell me if you're going as this Evie Frye. I may not recognize you," the girls laughed.

"I'll send you an Instagram," Shiree promised.

"Sooo last year," Kendra kidded. After Kendra left, Shiree sat on her bed and continued to search the internet. On a costume website, she thumbed through hundreds of images in their photo gallery, zipping through without even looking at most of them. Finally, she stopped and backed up a few pages.

"There you are," Shiree said to herself, "Evie Frye."

She was looking at a woman with a dark leather jacket over a black, silky undershirt. The form-fitting jacket extended past the waist. A short leather skirt fell low beneath the studded jacket. Leather metal-studded gloves extended to the elbows, and a long knife protruded from below the wrist of one hand. The model's black pants disappeared into the tops of calf-high leather boots. Black shoulder-length hair cascaded beneath a black hood. Shiree downloaded the picture and blew it up to a larger size.

Normal black formal gloves would do if she wrapped a studded leather wrist bracelet over them. She had a wide wrist bracelet already. She could easily apply fake studs with a rhinestone machine.

"She's got my hair already, and I've got most of this stuff except the fake knife," Shiree mused. "What does she do?"

Researching Assassin's Revenge, Shiree found the backstory for Evie Frye. She read everything she could find on the internet about Evie Frye. Shiree learned that Evie had a brother named Jacob, and they both were assassins, but not the bad kind. They were good assassins that fought for peace and liberty. They only assassinated criminals and fugitives. She looked at more pictures and thought she might talk her cousin into dressing up as Jacob. Both costumes would be simple to duplicate, she thought.

Shiree decided to learn all she could about Evie Frye. She downloaded the game and played for several hours. She got killed quickly the first few times she played but lasted longer as she learned her way around the game. Each time she would reboot, a different player would play the role of Jacob. It was never the same player twice so far. She enjoyed being able to roam the streets of Victorian London. The graphics were great but kind of dark and foggy. She wondered if it was realistic to what England really was. A couple of times, she got lost before she could even locate Jacob in the game.

Before turning out the light and going to bed, she restarted the game one more time and became even more engrossed. An hour later, she was still navigating foggy London streets looking for Jacob. A prompt appeared on the screen that gave her basic information about her mission, the positions of intended targets, and how to earn extra points. A small map showed her location in the city and indicated where she might find different characters.

Shiree knew from the earlier games to avoid the back alleys and bridges. After studying the map, she decided she needed to join forces with Jacob to survive. Rounding the corner, she came upon a group of thugs warming themselves over a fire burning in a trash barrel.

"Oh, no," she thought, "they're going to kill me again." Fortunately, the men only wanted to taunt her as she passed. Evie did not attempt to speak to any of them despite their attempts to engage her. As they faded behind her, she arrived at a bridge. She would need to cross to the other side. Evie had several options. She could walk across the bridge; she could take a ferry beneath the bridge, or she could hire a horse-drawn hack to take her to the other side. Shiree sensed that danger lurked on the bridge, so decided on the hack. It took most of the coins she had. Inside the hack, she found a purse some previous passengers had left behind. Inside were hundreds of coins. She needed the money, but when the cab stopped on the other side of the bridge, she climbed out and told the driver about the purse.

"Aye, Missy, you've found the missing purse, you 'ave! There's a reward, you know?"

"No, I didn't know," she typed into the response block.

"Well, there is, to yer great benefit. A more common person might 'ave kept the purse. The loser was the wife of the Constable. You're in luck. If you'd 'ave kept it, you'd 'ave been arrested for sure. But since ya' turned it over to me, I'm authorized to give you 'alf." Shiree watched as her coin count rose to ten times what she had before.

As Shiree moved through the game as Evie, more events happened. Some of them worked to her benefit, but some did not. At least she stayed alive and was able to continue looking for Jacob. Evie was getting close to where he should be. At the top of the screen, she noticed a little green light blinking. Not sure what to do, she clicked her mouse on the blinking light.

A window opened with a player profile for BuckineeR, who was playing as Jacob Frye. Shiree did not even know you could send messages within the game. BuckineeR was sending her a message. "Look out behind you," he warned.

Evie turned and saw a large man coming up behind her. He was one of the men from the burning barrel. The thug must have followed her here. He looked menacing and stared at her from the shadows. He knew she had money now. She looked at the small map and decided that Jacob must be very close. Evie took a chance and ducked down a short-cut alley that led more directly to where she thought Jacob was waiting. The stalker followed into the darkness of the lane. Evie picked up her pace, hoping to reach Jacob. Suddenly, a lasso dropped from the night above and caught the stalker by the legs, hoisting him high into the darkness. The green light blinked again.

"That was a close one," the message said.

"It sure was. Was that you?" Shiree typed.

"It was, my dear. I couldn't let anything happen to my sister, could I?" Jacob answered.

"Where are you?"

"You can meet me at the end of the alley. Just keep walking. Don't worry; you are safe now."

As Shiree and BuckineeR continued to text back and forth, the game receded into the background. After a while, BuckineeR's questions became more friendly and personal. "Where are you," he finally asked.

"Denver," Shiree replied. "You?"

"Wow! I'm in Denver, too!"

As they continued to text, Shiree found herself revealing some personal information, such as her real name and age. She did not give her e-mail address even though he asked.

"Are you going to Denver Comic-Con?" BuckineeR asked.

"Yes," Shiree replied. "I've decided to go as Evie Frye."

"I'll be there! Maybe we'll meet. You know Buck Russell will be there, don't you?"

"Who's Buck Russell?"

"Are you kidding me? Buck Russell is a famous Hollywood stunt man. He stunt doubles for Batman. Didn't you know that? His father is Mike Russell, a famous movie star!"

"I've heard of Mike Russell. I've seen a lot of his movies. Why is Buck coming to Comic-Con?"

"He's a featured celebrity. Look at the flyer. His name is on it."

Shiree opened another screen and checked. Buck Russell was a featured guest.

"I see him," she messaged BuckineeR. "Maybe I'll get to meet him."

"Yeah," BuckineeR replied, "as long as you've got $40. He'll be in a booth, and you can get his autograph for free, but if you want it on a picture, that will cost you 40 bucks."

"Oh," Shiree replied, disappointed.

"Don't worry," BuckineeR replied. "I know him – very well. Hint. Hint. I'll make sure you get to meet him."

"How will you find me in the crowd?" Shiree asked.

"There won't be many Evie Fries there. I'll find you."

"That would be fun." Shiree was thrilled. She noticed his profile name was "Buck," as in Buck Russell, maybe. Could BuckineeR really be the real Buck Russell?

BuckineeR messaged again. "I know Buck is filming a short feature for an upcoming video. If you are a convincing Evie Frye, maybe he'll put you in it. Can you send me a picture with your costume?"

"No, I can't do that. I'm sorry."

"It's okay," BuckineeR assured her. "I'm sure you look fetching."

"What about my friend, Kendra?"

"What's her costume?"

"Harley Quinn."

"Probably not, but she can watch. We'll need some extras."

Shiree noticed that he said, 'We'll need.' She was convinced she was talking to the real Buck Russell.

She could not wait to tell Kendra, but first, she had to make her costume – and it had to be good. She signed off the game with a promise to be back in touch with BuckineeR soon. Without her e-mail address, the only way they could communicate was inside the game. As she snuggled to her pillow, she dreamed of shooting a short video with the real Batman stunt double Buck Russell. In her dreams, Shiree swooned as Batman swooped in and saved her from the clutches of a horrible criminal.

# 7

When it was dark, Jack went to his garage and removed the cover from his white van. He opened the tailgate and made sure his equipment was inside; the toolbox, magnetic signs, and small parts were there. The registration and insurance papers were in the glove box. No room for error; everything must be perfect.

Jack was quite sure that no one in the neighborhood had ever seen the vehicle. He only drove it to Comic-Cons around the country, always leaving late at night. He kept the garage doors closed and the van covered. None of the nosy neighbors would ever be able to report seeing the vehicle at his home. Jack bought the truck with a wheelchair lift in Los Angeles for cash and drove it home late in the night a year ago.

One by one, he brought out his manikins and laid them in the rear compartment. They were fully dressed except for the footwear, which he stored in a separate box. There were five figures – three side-by-side and two on top. They looked like dead bodies lying there with their bare feet pointing up. Jack felt like putting a body tag on their toes for fun but decided that would be too bizarre. It might make someone talk. Jack did not want that. He covered the models with a blanket, making sure to tuck the end securely beneath the bare feet.

Jack loaded everything else into the back seats with his luggage on top. He checked the oil and fluid levels. With the tank more than three-quarters full, Jack realized a gas stop would be needed somewhere in the middle of Arizona. He thought he could make it to Flagstaff before he filled up. Jack had routed around Las Vegas, preferring to stick to the lonely desert at night. Just before Phoenix, he would turn north through the desert toward Flagstaff. It was a couple of hours longer that way, but Jack decided the area's remoteness was worth the extra time. The wouldn't be many people out in the middle of the night. He planned to stop somewhere around dawn and sleep during the day. It was better to travel only at night.

He made sure the wheelchair was secure, and the lift worked properly. All the tires had correct air pressure. Jack made one last trip through his house, making sure the timers for the lights were set correctly. He left the large living room big-screen on the news channel and turned on the back porch lights. Jack locked all the doors and set the alarm. He was ready to go. Before starting the van, Jack turned location tracking off on his cell phone and powered it down. Unwrapping his burner phone, he powered it on to make sure it worked and then quickly switched it off again. There was no need to turn it on until necessary.

Inside the van, he opened the garage door and rolled slowly down his driveway to the street, making sure the garage door came back down. No one was around. Perfect. He drove out of his subdivision and turned down the boulevard toward IH-8 East. There was a quarter moon shining behind the tall palms, casting a shadow on the street. Off to his left, the Pacific glistened in the moonlight. He passed only a few cars before he got to the freeway ramp. No one was behind him.

On the highway, Jack set the cruise control and scanned the radio for some music to his liking. He wished he had satellite radio, but he did not want anything that could track him. He had recorded some CDs in case there were no stations out in the desert.

Skirting the Mexican border past Los Algodones, Jack was glad when the Mexican border ran to the south. He followed the Colorado River into Yuma and headed deep into the dark desert. Jack was satisfied with the time reaching the turn-off at Gila Bend. He stopped in the desert and peed on the side of the road. Just after Palo Verde, Jack turned onto Arizona 303, avoiding Phoenix altogether. He hoped to make the outskirts of Flagstaff before the sun came up. He would find a motel and sleep through the daylight hours. The eastern sky was already growing pink.

Glancing at his gas gauge, Jack realized he would have to stop for gas. He did not have enough to make Flagstaff, and the last thing he wanted was to run out of gas. Rolling into New River, Arizona, Jack found an all-night station near the exit. No one was around, so he pulled on a pair of latex gloves and filled his van. At the window, he told the clerk he didn't want his hands to smell like gasoline.

As he pulled out of the station, Jack noticed a pair of parking lights blink on behind him. On the far side of the station, a police car sat unseen in the shadows. Jack peeled off the gloves and watched the police car follow him out onto the highway. It followed him at a distance along New River Road South. Jack reached beneath the seat, pulled out the gun, and stuck it in the holster beneath his arm under his jacket. Just before the city limits, the officer flipped on his red and blue lights. Jack cursed himself for not checking the service station closer before he pulled in.

Short of the city limits sign, Jack pulled his van over and snapped on his inside lights. He rolled down his windows, turned off his engine, and placed his hands in full sight on top of the steering wheel. The officer was slow getting out of his car, probably checking for warrants, he thought. Jack sat and waited.

Finally, the police car door opened as an officer emerged. Jack noted that no one else got out on the passenger side, so the cop was probably alone. You could never tell, though. Someone could be sitting in the passenger seat. Jack raised his left hand showing his fingers as the policeman eased up the passenger side of his van. The officer shined his light into the back windows and around the rear. He finally worked his way up to the passenger window and shined his flashlight in on Jack. Jack smiled at him.

"Sir, may I see your license and registration?"

"Yes, sir, no problem ... uh, my registration is in the glove box, and my license is in my pocket."

"You have any weapons in the car or anything I should know about?"

"No, sir," Jack lied.

"Go ahead then and open your glove box for the registration. I'll take that first."

Jack reached over and opened the box. The officer shined his light inside and watched as Jack brought out the paperwork.

"Okay, now, if you will close the glove box, please get your license from your pocket."

The policeman took his license and registration back to his patrol unit as Jack sat and waited. Jack watched in the rearview mirror and saw that no one was in the officer's passenger seat. Eventually, the officer came back with Jack's paperwork on a clipboard. He was on the driver's side this time.

"Mr. Russell, I'm Officer Johnson of the New River Police Department. Do you have any idea why I pulled you over?"

"Call me Buck," Jack smiled. "No, sir, I know I wasn't speeding. I just left a station back there where I filled up with gas."

"Where are you going this time of night?"

"I'm going to Denver. I prefer to drive at night."

"It's kind of out of your way from LA to Denver, isn't it? You didn't go I-15 to 70 west?"

"No," Jack shook his head. "I had to stop at Phoenix first. Girlfriend – you know how it is," Jack laughed. "Actually, I plan to hit I-40 at Flagstaff by daylight."

"Do you know your license plate light is out?"

"No! Really? No, I did not know that. Look, I have a spare bulb and a screwdriver in the back, and I'll be happy to change it right now, if that's okay."

"If you don't mind, why don't you pull into that parking lot over there to change it then? Do you need any help?"

"I can do it, but maybe you can hold the flashlight for me."

"Sure, I can do that," the officer nodded.

Son-of-a-bitch just wants to see what's in the back, Jack knew. No problem; I've got nothing illegal. Just be friendly and let him look. Jack pulled to the curb and opened the tailgate as he rummaged around for a spare bulb. He was glad he had brought the spare parts kit.

The cop shined his light all around the back of Jack's van. Jack had to reach farther inside to reach the screwdriver. He intentionally pushed the blanket up as he stretched, exposing one of the manikin's feet. The officer stepped back quickly and pulled his gun.

"Put your hands on the side of the vehicle! Now!" Jack stretched his arms across the rear door, showing that his hands were empty. "What the hell is that?" the cop shouted, staring at the exposed foot in his spotlight.

"It's just a model," Jack assured him. "It's a dummy."

"Mr. Russell, move over there by the side of the road and keep your hands where I can see them."

Jack did as instructed as the cop reached inside and squeezed the vinyl foot. He pulled back the blanket and saw the other dolls staring up at him.

"Holy shit, there's more of them! What are you doing driving around with a van full of dummies?"

"Officer Johnson, you don't know who I am, do you?"

"Your license says, Buck Russell. Is that who you are?"

"Yes, sir, I'm him. If you don't recognize me, that's okay. I'm in the movies. Actually, I'm a stunt double for Batman – or whoever's playing Batman at the time."

"Guess that explains why all the figures are dressed up like superheroes."

"Yep, I'm going to Denver Comic-Con to set up a display. I'll be signing autographs, too. I'll be glad to sign one for you if you like."

"Batman, huh?"

"That's right."

"You scared the hell out of me. Dead bodies in a trunk in the middle of the night – come on!" The officer began to relax as he realized Jack was not a threat. "Yeah, I can't wait to tell my kid I pulled Batman over."

"What's your kid's name?" Jack asked as he scribbled Buck Russell on a photograph and handed it to Officer Johnson."

After the lamp was changed and the officer left, Jack placed the bone-handled revolver back under the seat. He was going to have to stop soon and layover. The sky had changed from a soft pink to a reddish peach. Daylight was coming on fast. He laughed as he drove, thinking of the cop. He was glad he had not attached the body tags.

# 8

Selma found Papa Joe right where Stephen said he would be – behind the Pig Stand. Papa Joe had a chair placed in the shade of the overpass formed by the flyover from 281 and I-35. It was a cool, shady spot with lots of grass and small shade trees. The city kept it mowed, and the cops kept it cleaned out of bums for the most part. If the bums didn't trash the place out and didn't stay too long, some of the officers would turn a blind eye. Papa Joe was careful not to give the appearance of being too permanent. All he had was an HEB grocery basket full of odds and ends he had picked up around the streets.

Selma had to park near the cafe, so she had to walk across a wide expanse of grass to get to him. The old man wore a slouch hat and sported a bandaged left arm hanging from a soiled sling. Selma noticed he had a white gauze bandage on the left side of his head. As Selma approached, she watched Papa Joe stash a wine bottle into a beat-up old green gym bag next to his chair.

Papa Joe shielded his eyes with a dirty hand as Selma approached. "You tha po-po?" He asked.

"Yes, sir," Selma showed her badge. "Are you Papa Joe?"

"Well, you're a right pretty one, though, if you don't mind me sayin' so."

"Thank you, Papa Joe."

"I didn't say I was Papa Joe," he said with a sly grin.

"Oh," Selma admitted, "no, you didn't. Are you Papa Joe?" Selma knew she was going to have to butter up this old codger.

"Who wants to know?"

"Sorry, you caught me off guard with the flattery," Selma claimed. "My name is Detective Cibolo with the San Antonio Police Department."

"What you want with Papa Joe – if'n I do see him?"

"I heard he got hit by a car a few nights ago, and I was just following up on the report. Was that you?"

"Damn right, it was me! That damned ambulance near 'bout took my head off – crazy bastard. Knocked me into a damned ditch over yonder," Papa Joe pointed. "Laid there all night. I could'a died."

"That's what I came to talk to you about. How are you feeling now? I see they got you bandaged up and everything."

"Feelin' okay, considering," Papa Joe rubbed his head. "I'm suin' the damn city for a million dollars, soon's I get me a damned lawyer."

"I'll try to help you with that, Papa Joe."

Papa Joe was skeptical. "Why would you wanna help me?" he asked. "You tha city."

"Because by helping you, it might help us. We want to know who was driving that ambulance – same as you do. I'll share my information with you if you tell me what you know."

"Can't hurt," Papa Joe admitted suspiciously as he rubbed the crusty side of his drooping mustache.

"Can you describe the ambulance? What color was it? Did it have any name on the side?"

Papa Joe scratched his head and tried to remember. "It was all white – I know that. I recall there was a name on the side, but I can't remember what it was."

"White? Are you sure, Papa Joe?"

"Damn right! Pert near left white skid marks on the side of my head! All's I could see when I was fallin' was that white bat-outta-hell runnin' me down. It was white – I know it was."

"Did you see who was driving? Can you describe the driver at all?"

"Naw," Papa Joe admitted. "It was too dark, and he was movin' fast. I didn't get no look at him at all."

Selma opened a notebook she had brought with pictures of all the emergency units operating in San Antonio. There was a mixture of colors; red, blue, green, orange, and yellow, but no solid white. She flipped through so Papa Joe could see.

"Well, this one was white, I tell you. Like snow, and it clipped me a good one right on my shoulder and my forehead. White, I tell you! It was white!"

Selma turned to the last page of the notebook and started flipping forward toward the front. The care cabs and transport units were filed back there, and some of them were white except for the logos.

"There it is!" Papa Joe suddenly shouted and stabbed his forefinger into the page. "That's the sum-bitch that ran me down – right there!"

"You recognize the unit? This is the actual one?"

"One like it, then. Just like it."

"But, Papa Joe, this is a wheelchair van, not an ambulance."

"Same thing," he insisted. "Damn thing like to killed me. It was that kind of ambulance."

"You're sure?"

"Yes, sir-ree-Bob, I'm sure. I'm gonna sue that sum-bitch too!"

"Well, Papa Joe, that is not one of the city's units. All of ours are white on the top with big red bands around the bottom. You would have seen red."

"There weren't no red, I told you. It was white – all white."

"I understand, Papa Joe. Here is what I can tell you. I don't think you were hit by a city emergency vehicle. I think it was a private wheelchair van."

"Not the city?"

"No, sir. I don't think so. None of our units are solid white."

"You're not jus' sayin' that so I don't sue your ass off – pardon the bad language, ma'am."

"No, sir, I wouldn't do that."

"Well, who then?" Papa Joe asked. "Who'm I gonna sue?"

"I don't know, Papa Joe. I don't know."


The Blue Line Lounge is a cop bar off S. Presa Street. It was formerly known as the "Shift Change," but the new owner wanted to show support for the police department. The cops like the place, and because the regulars are either current or former police officers, the bar didn't get many other visitors. Most cops go there after their shift to unwind by knocking back a couple and spinning stories and lies about their most recent calls.

The Blue Line was a hole-in-the-wall dump, but it has a clear view of the street-front parking and a back-alley door. It made a handy hang-out if you wanted to lay low after a shift or to hide out for any reason. As soon as you stepped inside, you could tell it was a cop bar. Stragglers usually didn't stay long and ambled out almost as soon as they came in. The bare cement floors always seemed damp and looked like they had been swamped out with a power washer. The place was a total dive, but the cops didn't care. What you could see of the cement walls had not been cleaned or dusted in years. Police mementos lined the walls, including some that probably should have been in the evidence room. A well-stocked bar lined the front part, where Floyd, a former policeman, usually tended bar. Brenda and Dotty kept the tables well supplied with refills in draft glasses, cans, or long neck bottles.

Over the years, Floyd and others were presented numerous dubious awards prominently displayed on the walls amid hundreds of pictures of cops in various stages of inebriation. One wall was dedicated to fallen heroes, and the names and photos of police and other first responders were proudly displayed along with a flag.

The back room wasn't much cleaner, but it contained two well-used pool tables. Beneath an antique Pearl Beer light that hung low over the green felt playing surface, Selma lined up the black eight ball in the corner pocket and slammed it in. She picked up the two dollars lying on the table and stuffed them in her pocket.

"Want to go again? She asked Bran as she reached for the rack sitting in a slot at the end of the table.

"No, I've had enough," Bran laughed. "You want another beer?"

Selma scooped up the quarters lined up on the edge of the pool table and sat down at a table in the corner while Bran went up front to get the beer. There was no one else in the back room. Selma leaned her elbows on the table and placed her head in her hands. She only looked up when Bran put the cold can in front of her.

"I've about had it, too, Bran," Selma mused.

"Oh, not that, again," Bran moaned.

"I know you're tired of hearing it," Selma nodded, "but I'm serious. There has to be a better way to make a living. Maybe I'm just not cut out for police work."

"Come on," Bran smiled. "You can't mean that. Look at all you've done. You're the youngest person ever to pass the detective exam and the youngest detective on the force. You're going to be Chief someday. Just stick it out."

"I don't know," Selma shook her head. "I don't think I fit in here. Thorn won't give me the time of day, and I'm too restricted in what he lets me do. It's just one cold case after another. I'm tired of feeling out of place."

"What would you do if he gave you your head? What would you do differently?"

"Bran, I'm convinced that girl in the dumpster had something to do with Comic-Con. Something tells me that – I don't know. It wasn't just a casual pickup or someone she knew. This girl was abducted from the Civic Center."

"Someone took her out right in front of 5,000 people?" Bran asked.

Selma looked directly into Bran's blue eyes, "Yeah," Selma nodded. "Yeah. He took her out in front of all those people – somehow."

"She had to go willingly. If she set up a fight, someone would have stepped in or reported it."

"I guess so," she admitted. "Come on, let's go. I'll buy you a burger," Selma stood.

Bran quickly stepped in front of her. "Let's go out the back," he suggested.

"Why? We're parked upfront."

"No reason. I just thought we could use the walk –"

"Why would we want to walk all the way around the building, Bran? That's stupid." Selma moved toward the opening between the rooms. She could hear Thorn's loud voice before she could see him.

"… chasin' Batman," he laughed. "I told her we're not chasin' Batman down some rabbit hole."

The entire room whooped with laughter. "Maybe it was Robin," someone added. Selma stood in the doorway as the laughter sounded in her ears. Thorn was in fine form as he went through a litany of Selma's theories on the murders. "We might call him the Comic-Con Killer," he blurted as the room responded with raucous laughter.

Selma stood in the doorway, listening to the others making fun of her. She held out her hand to prevent Bran from squeezing past to warn the others. "No," she whispered, "let's see what they've got to say."

"She's like a Barbie Doll with a badge," Thorn hooted, and the room ate it up. "It could be worse," someone shouted back. "I'll take a Barbie Doll over the Goat Woman anytime," the others chimed in.

Eventually, one of the officers noticed her, and red-faced, he nodded toward the back room. "What?" Thorn bellowed, "Is she behind me or something?" Thorn snickered, thinking it was a joke. "I fell for that last time," he guffawed.

"Pardon me, gentlemen," Selma said to a quickly sobering Thorn. "You too, Thorn. I'm sorry; I didn't mean to interrupt your fun," she said as she walked quickly through the bar and out the front door. A few shame-faced men called after her, "Come on, Selma. Stay. We were just horsing around." She ignored their pleas, trying to get to the sidewalk as quickly as she could.

"You ass!" Bran blasted Thorn as he followed Selma outside.

# 9

Selma was near the end of her rope. She still refused to play the victim card. It was probably not even a good idea to be venting to Bran the evening before. However, she trusted him not to take it any further than just the two of them. Sometimes, you needed someone to blow off some steam. Her exit did not make things any better. There were some red faces and downcast eyes all around as she stomped out of the Blue Line. She got it; she was not one of them. She also understood that they needed to decompress just as much as she did. She realized that most of them were embarrassed. She probably should have stayed and laughed with them, but it hurt too bad. She had spent her time on the streets, and she knew that cops had difficulty apologizing. She didn't expect an apology. Selma had spent enough time in uniform to understand what was happening. It was someone's time in the barrel, and tonight was her time. She decided they were not going to run her off. If she needed to leave, she was going to leave on her power. However, now was not the time, and this was not the reason. Still, it burned.

Before leaving for work, she sat at her kitchen table with her coffee considering her next approach. She went over her notes and became even more convinced that the Comic-Con had something to do with Hanna's death. But how could she convince Thorn to let her follow up on those leads? She thought of asking for a hearing from the Captain but decided against that. She would gain nothing by going over Thorn's head except greater resentment. She asked herself why she was so convinced it involved Comic-Con – what were her main points? She scribbled some notes and left for the station, deciding to try to get Thorn's ear one more time before she went upstairs to the Captain. She was not going rouge; she would ask Thorn for permission to take her case to a higher level before she did. Maybe that would convince him she was loyal. She hoped.

Selma realized that there were upper-level expectations of her. Sure, she had earned the promotion, and it was an adjustment period for everyone. The future of all those young women who came behind her depended on her success. She was not about to wimp out and throw in the towel now. The weight of that responsibility was too heavy for her just to give up. Too many people depended upon her to get it right. Besides, she was proud of her record. She wanted to be a homicide detective. She knew she was not Thorn's choice, but then, he was not her choice either. One way or another, they had to forge their path through this clutter to get to a workable solution. Thorn had already mentioned how management was leaning on him to accept the changes. Bringing new heat down on him now was not going to make things any better.

Maybe this was a good time to get Thorn to listen to her. Thorn might not agree with her theories, but maybe, after last night, he might feel embarrassed enough to let her talk it out with him. All she could do right now was hope he would listen. She walked in with her brightest smile and sat behind her desk. Thorn was pretending to read, but he was watching her over the top of his computer screen. He had that guilty, deer-in-the-headlights look, not knowing what Selma was going to do next. What she did was go over and sat in the chair in front of Thorn's desk.

"Before you start …" Thorn began to speak.

"No," Selma put up her hands. "No need. No apologies. I get it. I've been in those bull sessions before too. All I ask is that you give me five minutes of your time. Five uninterrupted minutes to say what I've got to say without you coming back with excuses or talking down to me. Can I have that?"

Thorn sat upright in his chair, "You're not going to quit, are you?"

"Hell, no! What do you think – I haven't heard that crap before? I've heard that and a lot worse. It's just cops being cops. What I want is a fair chance to make my case. Can I have that? Five minutes to explain what I'm thinking. Can't you just let me have that, Thorn? Five minutes?"

Thorn nodded, "That's fair," he agreed.

"Thorn, I know you don't agree with my theories on that murder of the girl in the dumpster ==."

"Are we still on that?" Thorn began.

Selma held up her finger. "Five minutes," she reminded him. "Thorn, I know it is a changing world. Technology changes every day. The internet gets bigger every minute. Video gaming is a big part of that. Do you know some 18-year-olds make over a million dollars a year on video games?"

Thorn was shocked, "A mill—" he started before Selma's finger went up again.

"More money than that for some of them. There are more than two hundred realistic action games you can play. This one particular game I want to talk to you about,

Assassin's Revenge, has been downloaded over 40-million times."

Thorn's forehead wrinkled as he tried to come to grips with the size of it, "40 mill—" Up went Selma's finger.

"I still have four and a half minutes," she reminded him. "This girl was dressed up like a character from that game – Evie Frye. Let me tell you about that game. It is super violent. There are more killings per second in that game than in the entire world. They try to make the games as real as possible. Young people get addicted to them. Parents either don't care, or they are too busy to check what their child is doing. Even if they do pay attention, it is billed as a safe way to vent adolescent aggression. These games get their adrenalin running. Parents, who grew up with Pac-Man and Donkey Kong, think their kids are home, in a safe environment. What could go wrong?"

"This particular game, Assassin's Revenge, involves killing the bad guys before they kill you. The game has street scenes right out of Victorian London. If you play, you can wander around the ancient streets, see actual buildings, and even talk to people from that era. It is very impressive. Imagine the research these designers did to build the game. Sometimes, it is almost like you are really there."

"This girl, Hannah Gleason, was dressed like Evie Frye when we found her. Let me tell you about Evie Frye. She was no lightweight little girl. She is a cold-blooded killer. She has a brother who is just as bad, and together, they knock off most of the storied villains of that period. The twist is Evie and Jacob were the good ones. They were the ones keeping the world safe from Jack the Ripper type of villains."

"Did you ever wonder why Comic-Con was such a big deal? It is the one place where these young people, some not so young, can go dressed as their favorite character, and no one thinks anything about it. Have you ever been to one? Comic-Con brings in hundreds of thousands of dollars to the City. How do you think they can afford to rent the Civic Center? These characters spend a lot of money. When they dress the part, they call it "cosplay" – costume play. It is like Halloween, only with characters from comic books and games. You've probably seen them on the streets going in and out of the Civic Center during the event. You probably thought they were weirdos or something, but they are not. They are normal high-school and college kids playing the part of their favorite superhero."

"These games are so addictive; some players would rather be in the game than in their real world. They spend more and more time online, ignoring their real lives, skipping family events, piling up bad grades, and walking around sleep-deprived. They want to be the characters they portray in the game. They stop studying, drop out of college, and lose their jobs over lack of sleep. Is it so hard to believe that under the right circumstances, some mentally disturbed individual might take it too far?"

Thorn did not respond. He was deep in thought as the points Selma made sank deep into his awareness.

Selma continued, "Thorn, what if somebody who was already mentally unstable decided he **was** one of those characters?"

"Like Batman?" Thorn asked. "Batman is not a killer, Selma."

"No, Thorn, Batman is not a killer. Neither is Wonder Woman or Superman, but there are others, Thorn. Others you know nothing about – vicious scoundrels, villains, and anti-heroes who are killers. What if a psycho thought the game was real, and his life was a game? What would he do? You should see some of these costumes, Thorn. They walk around with giant hammers, swords, knives, and even evil-looking hatchets like executioners used in the old days."

"Real ones?" Thorn's eyebrows raised.

"No, plastic replicas," Selma assured him.

"Well, they can't kill many people with plastic swords," Thorn laughed.

"No, but some of them are so realistic, you can't tell a real one from a fake," Selma assured him. "Some of them even have fake blood smeared on the blades. You wouldn't be able to tell a fake knife from a real one at a distance," Selma assured him.

Thorn had had enough. "Okay, I've listened. Are you done?"

"Yeah, but can't you at least understand what I'm trying to tell you?"

"First, the victim was not stabbed, chopped up, or beaten with a hammer. In fact, she didn't have a mark on her." Thorn handed her a sheaf of papers. "Coroner's report; natural causes," he said. "She had asthma."

"In the second place, thank you for telling me all of this. I'm glad I listened – I learned something. I did." Thorn leaned back in his chair and sighed. "Go ahead and check your hunches out if you want. I'm not buying it much, but you never know what a nut case will do. You may be on to something for all I know."

Selma nodded, "Thanks."

"How did he get her out?" Thorn asked.

"What?"

"How did a maniacal killer get a 17-year old girl out of a building with 5,000 people watching?"

"I haven't figured that out yet," Selma admitted.

"Well, you keep on figuring. In my experience, what happened was: she went there alone; hooked up with a boy; they go out joyriding; making out in the park; she has an asthma attack; he panics; she dies, and he dumps her and runs. Isn't that just as possible?"

"Yeah. It's plausible," Selma had to agree.

"One more thing," Thorn leaned forward. "About last night – no, don't brush it off. I was wrong. I owe you an apology. You are better than that. I was just seething about a lot of things. I had a few too many, and I took it out on you."

"I know that – we've all been there, Thorn. That's not the problem."

"What's the problem? I treat you like everyone else. I don't open doors or pull out chairs for you? I don't treat you like a woman? What?"

Selma blinked. "No."

"Then, what?"

Selma looked at him and hated the moistness in her eyes. She softly said, "You didn't treat me like a partner."

# 10

A white van pulled slowly into the Walmart parking lot in Flagstaff. Walmart has long been a safe-haven for travelers. It had been a long night, and he was tired. That cop in Arizona had slowed him down, so it was already daylight. He still had ten hours to drive before he reached Denver. He planned to sleep all day and move on after the sun went down. Jack parked in the far corner to not be a nuisance to shoppers and set up the reflective windshield covers. Safe in his vehicular cocoon, he thought about his plan to lure Shiree to Comic-Con the next day.

He had little to do but made himself comfortable in the seat in the back by the wheelchair. Pulling out his tablet, he logged in and switched to his virtual private network. He had defaulted the privacy settings to turn off all location detection. With this setup, he felt safe and confident that no one would know where he was located.

Jack signed in to his streaming movie account and watched his favorite mystery series until he got tired. He ate from an ice-chest he had prepared in advance. There was no chance anyone would see him until he was ready. No security camera would catch his image and give a clue to his whereabouts later. Late in the afternoon, when he thought school was out, he turned off the movie channel and started playing Assassin's Revenge. Signing in as BuckineeR, he selected his normal avatar, Jacob Frye, and looked for Evie.

He almost reached Evie, but another player eliminated him before he could get to her location. Signing out, he turned off his tablet and logged in again. This time, he avoided elimination and was able to locate Evie rather quickly. He checked the player's profile and discovered it was a player named China. Not the right one. He abandoned the game and reloaded it again.

Jack found Evie Frye's in New York, Dallas, and London, but no Shiree in Denver. After an hour, Jack was getting frustrated. Jack required anonymity. Jack had done some research and found Shiree's e-mail address on her social media page. He decided he would e-mail her if that were the only way. It was dangerous, and it left a trail to follow for the cops, but he thought he had covered his tracks well enough. Chatting inside the game provided more secrecy, but Jack couldn't take the chance she might not show up.

Firing up the game once more, Jack finally found Shiree playing as Evie Frye. He followed her in the game for another hour, taking out opponents several times before she got into trouble. He wanted to wait for her to message him first. That would make her feel safer. If she didn't message soon, he'd use the e-mail. After he cleared the way for her one more time, Jack smiled as the little green message light began to blink.

"Tks," Shiree typed.

"NP," Jack answered. "You Shiree from Denver?" he asked.

"Hi, Buck."

"Hello, darlin'," he typed. "U still goin' to Comic-Con tomorrow?"

"OFC"

"Well, guess what?"

"What?" Shiree asked.

"I got you in the video!"

"GR8! Tks."

"NP. Say, can you send me a picture of you in costume so that I can give it to the producer?"

"No can do. Promised momma."

"Got it. NP. Anyway, you are in. Will you be there around closing?"

"Going down on the bus with Kendra. We'll stay until closing."

"Ok. Meet me in the refreshment area near the loading dock. I'll explain the gig then. Ok?"

"Ok. Kendra, too?"

"Sure, but she's not in the scene – just an extra."

"She'll be disappointed."

"Sorry – not my call. Are you in?"

"Yes! I'll be there. How will I know you?"

"I'll be dressed as Spring-heeled Jack."

"Who's that? I thought you were Jacob or Batman."

"Usually, but not this time."

"Who is he?"

"Look him up. Besides, I'll find you. You'll know me as BuckineeR."

"What time?"

"Five pm. G2G, CYaL8er."

"I'll be there," Shiree promised.

Then he was gone. Shiree signed off the game and began to read about Spring-heeled Jack. She was enthralled at what she read. She could see it in her mind's eye.


Mary Stevens worked her way along the darkened streets of London one night in 1837. The shadows in the dark places were creepy and chilling. She tried to keep to the light, but the gas lamps were not strong enough to light the entire walkway between brick buildings. After visiting her parents in Battersea, she returned to a house on Lavender Hill, where she worked as a servant. Mary was happy to be nearing the end of her journey. She tugged her shawl closer around her neck and hastened her steps. Walking past Clapham Common, a figure leaped at her from the dark. The ghostly figure caught Mary in a powerful grasp and began kissing her face and tearing at her clothing with his claws. When Mary screamed, residents emerged from their houses as the attacker ran away. Despite a chase, the attacker disappeared into the darkness. Witnesses reported the dark, mysterious attacker leaped a wall taller than his head.

A few days later, Mary read in the papers that the assailant assaulted another pedestrian on next night, near where the attacker grabbed her. In this case, the newspaper did not identify the victim. The mugger leaped from a very tall wall and held his victim in much the same manner as he grabbed Mary. Again fleeing the scene, he jumped in front of a carriage, which caused the coachman to lose control and crash. The accident severely injured the coachman, requiring his hospitalization, while the dark figure escaped by jumping over a 9-foot wall.

Such stories became commonplace as the press began to identify the villain as Spring-heeled Jack due to his remarkable leaping ability. Mary Stevens avoided that area completely for the rest of her life, and she was never attacked again.

On January 9, 1838, the Lord Mayor of London, Sir John Cowan, called a public meeting in Mansion House, London, concerning reports of attacks on local women. Dozens of distressed residents attended, hoping to end the horrendous attacks. The Mayor read an anonymous message from a "resident of Peckham" that described attacks in which several ladies have been deprived of their senses, with two likely never to recover. The Mayor was skeptical of these reports, but several in attendance swore that the incidents were factual. The Times carried accounts of the hearing, and several other journals of the day covered the story. It was further reported that several young women in Hammersmith were frightened into "dangerous fits," and some of the women were bloodied by the beast's claws.

The Mayor was unconvinced. It seemed impossible that the accused stalker could perform such super-human feats described by various witnesses. He concluded that the witnesses and victims were exaggerating. Despite his doubts, the stories spread and grew. By April, the newspapers were referring to all such attacks as the work of Spring-heeled Jack. The assaults on Lucy Scales and Jane

Alsop heightened the tension and caused widespread fear among the residents.

In February 1838, Jane Alsop reported that she answered the door at her father's house to a man claiming to be the police. He excitedly asked her to bring a light, as he had caught the infamous Spring-heeled Jack in an alley across the way. She fetched him a lantern to the street. Upon receiving it, the assailant immediately threw off his cloak, revealing a fearsome figure who belched blue and white flames from his mouth. His eyes resembled red balls of fire. Without saying a word, the criminal began to tear her gown with his claws. Screaming, Jane ran back toward the house, where her sister appeared to help her. The monster fled the scene before other residents could be summoned. Jane suffered from scratches and claw marks around the neck and shoulders.

A little more than a week later, 18-year-old Lucy Scales was returning home with her sister after visiting her brother. Her brother was a well-known butcher who lived in a respectable section of Limehouse. In her deposition to police, Lucy stated that she and her sister were passing Green Dragon Alley when they saw a figure in the shadows. Lucy was walking ahead of her sister, and when she came even with the stranger, who wore a large dark cloak, he spat blue flame into her face, blinding her as she fell to the ground. A few blocks away, Lucy's brother heard the screams of his sisters and sprinted to the scene. He found Lucy on the pavement in a fit of fear, supported by her sister attempting to calm her. The brother carried her home while his other sister told him what had happened. The sister described the assailant as being tall, thin, and covered in a huge cloak.

Within the week, a man named Thomas Millbank bragged in a pub that he was Spring-heeled Jack. The police took his claim so seriously that the constable arrested him and hauled him before a judge at Lambath Street Court. He only escaped conviction because Jane Alsop swore he breathed fire, and Millbank admitted that he could do no such thing.

Spring-heeled Jack began to appear in penny pamphlets and plays held in the lower-level theaters of the day. As his fame grew, Spring-heeled Jack's appearances became fewer and fewer. He reappeared in 1843 as reports of attacks of drivers of mail carriages swept the area. By the 1870s, media frenzy resulted in more sightings and even gunfire aimed at suspicious appearances. Spring-heeled Jack's legend continued to grow as reports that he was impervious to bullets began to circulate.

In the end, the Legend of Spring-heeled Jack lived much longer than his human counterpart could possibly have lived. Jack gradually dissolved into a folk character, much the same as Bigfoot or Yeti.

Shiree's imagination ran wild. What if Hollywood was going to do a movie about Spring-heeled Jack, staring Buck Russell? Would Shiree, as Evie Frye, be lucky enough to be part of that film project? Shiree could not wait to find out. There was no way she was going to miss her appointment with BuckineeR.

# 11

Selma settled behind her desk for a long day of entering cold case files into the updated central filing system. The new system was going to be much better than lugging those hard copy files around. She opened the dark plumb-colored file at the top of the stack and found data on another murder victim. She was a young woman, aged 20, whose body was found near Brackenridge Park. October 30, 2016. The night before Halloween. Selma wrote the date on her pad. On a whim, she opened her web search page and typed in 2016 San Antonio Comic-Con. Selma's heart raced as she stared at the result with a sense of awe. The dates for the San Antonio Comic-Con were October 27-30, 2016.

She flipped to the back of the folder to look at the crime scene photos but found nothing there. The investigating detective was Sgt. Howard Burns. She glanced at her list of PD employees. The list did not contain Detective Burns. Thorn was out of the office, so she could not ask him. She finished reading the file and visited one of the other homicide detective teams across the hall.

Detective Phillips sat at a wooden desk, typing into the file system from an old file similar to the one Selma had in her hand. He had propped his folder up against his monitor.

"Hey, Mike," Selma greeted him, "whatcha doin'?"

Mike looked up and scowled, "Same as you. I'm stuck in here updating these old cold case files. I'll be glad when this is over and everything is digitized. I hate this crap."

Selma laughed, "I thought I was the only one."

"Nah, we all have to do it. I'd rather be out huntin' down bad guys than in here punching this keyboard."

"Me, too," Selma agreed. "I wonder why they are making us do it? Why didn't they just turn it over to central admin?"

"They did!" Make carped. "But there are piles and piles of these old files. They gave us the latest five years and turned a truckload over to admin. I'm serious: an entire truckload. They are probably as tired of it as we are. I'll bet they have a hundred years of files."

"Wow! That's a lot of work. I don't feel so bad now. Say! Do you know a detective that used to work here named Burns?"

"Old Burnie?"

"I guess so – his name was Howard Burns."

"Yeah, that's him. Sure! I knew Burnie. He retired a year or so ago. Worked on Sgt. Hoyle's team – he'd know more about Burnie than I would."

Selma made a note. "Mike, do you have any idea why the crime scene photos might be missing from one of his files?"

"I don't know; Old Burnie wasn't the best at record keeping. Just between you and me, I heard retirement was not his idea. The brass finally got tired of his sloppy work. He was out of here in a week, but that's just scuttlebutt."

"Where do you think the pictures might be?"

"If they're not in the file, I have no idea."

Hoyle heard them talking as he passed in the hall and poked his head in the door. "Come on in, Sarge," Mike waved him in. Hoyle dropped into the offered chair as Selma got right to the point.

"Sargent, do you remember a detective named Howard Burnes?"

Hoyle slumped his head down to his chest. "What's he done now?" he asked dejectedly.

"I don't know, Sergeant. I thought he was retired."

"He is. Why are you asking about him? Is there a problem with another case he worked on? What am I asking for?" Hoyle laughed, "With Burnie, there is always a problem. What is it this time?"

"I'm going through a case a couple of years old, and I can't find the crime scene photos."

"Well, I'm not surprised. Burnie's case files were a mess. Sometimes we would even find evidence in his bottom desk drawer. Once, he lost an entire file. We didn't even know it until years later. No record – nothing! Captain almost fired him on the spot for that one. He was a mess! He'd have stuff in the trunk of his car. Hell, I heard he had stuff in his garage at home. If those pictures aren't in the file, there ain't no telling where they are."

Selma returned to her office and read as much as she could of the old murder. Stuck on the back of one of the divider pages was a yellow sticky note. Someone had written the address 2321 Hwy 17, Lytle. She quickly looked the address up on a map. It was a farmhouse out in the sticks of the southwestern part of Bexar County. The city straddled Bexar, Atascosa, and Medina Counties. The farmhouse was in the Medina County part – out of Selma's jurisdiction.

When her shift was over, Selma stuffed the file into her bag and left the office. It was one of those summer days when the heat rose into huge bulbous clouds that turned purple and dark blue against the pale western sky. Globs of white cumulous clouds covered the rest of the sky. Selma could smell rain in the air.

After dinner, Selma sat on her couch, flipping channels. She could not get the missing photos out of her mind. She opened the file and looked at the sticky note with the address again. Whose address was this? She knew it was not the victim's address; Burnie had recorded that information in the file. Why was it in the file? Maybe it was a witness.

Outside, the rain shower was over, so Selma slipped on a pair of jeans and a pullover. There was one way to find out, she thought as she grabbed her car keys. It was already dark outside. She dropped the file folder on the passenger seat and started the car. Driving south on I-35, Selma noted that the rain was not completely over. The smell of rain and dirt filled the air. The sky was still dark with heavy clouds. Streaks of lightning lit up the dusky sky that filled the horizon in front of her.

In just over half an hour, Selma pulled off the interstate toward the town of Lytle. She slowed in front of an aging farmhouse on Highway 17. Aiming her flashlight at a rusty mailbox, Selma read "Burns," barely visible on the side. The address in the file was Burnie's house. Why would he write his own address down, she wondered. She looked up the muddy gravel driveway at the frame house set back off the road. A white van stood in front of the house, but she could see no inside lights. In the back, there was an outdoor halogen security light over a barn door. Selma decided to drive up to the house, despite the "No Trespassing" sign nailed to the front gate.

Her tires made a crunching sound as she rolled down the drive. No one came out, and no lights came on. The rundown house looked like it belonged in a horror movie. The place needed some work. No one had cared for the lawn in years. Long strings of Spanish moss hung from the oak trees like a witch's hair. As she got closer, Selma was able to see paint peeling from the outside walls.

Selma parked her car next to the white van parked in front. She was surprised that no dogs came out to greet her or to warn her away. Walking around the truck, Selma noted the California plates and the wheelchair lift on the passenger side. Selma was careful to keep her flashlight on as she climbed the rickety steps of the house. Lightning flashed in the distance, and the light bounced off the wall and across the floor of the porch.

Knocking on the door, she saw the light go on in a back room down a long hallway. After a while, a male voice spoke to her through the door. "Who is it?" He barked. "What do you want?"

"I'm Selma Cibolo – I'm looking for Howard. Is he here?"

There was a long pause before the answer came, "He's dead."

"Oh! I didn't know. I'm so sorry," Selma replied. "I had no idea. Is Mrs. Burns here?"

"She's dead too."

"Oh, my gosh. I apologize. I really didn't know. Who am I talking to, please?"

"Who wants to know?"

"As I said, I'm Selma. I work for the San Antonio Police Department. I'm a detective like Howard."

The door creaked open a crack as a tall, dark man peered through the screen. "I'm Jack," he stated. "Did you work with my dad?"

"No, we worked for the same department, though."

"What d'ya want?"

"I'm looking for some files he may have had before he died. I'm working on a case, and there would have been some pictures and reports and stuff. Would you know where he might keep something like that? It's very important."

"Do you have a warrant?" Jack asked.

"No. I was hoping your Howard might be here, and he might be willing to share them with me. I'm sorry to disturb you. I'm just looking for documents, that's all. Nothing against your father – it's just I thought he might still have some of those old records."

Jack stepped through the screened doorway and looked Selma over. He was a tall, dark man dressed in black clothing. He had a black hoodie over his head that covered the sides of his face. A black, short beard bristled on his cheeks and chin.

"You got a light there," he pointed at Selma's flashlight. "You might find some stuff in the barn out back. It's unlocked. You can go look. He had a kind of office back there – you'll see it when you go in. There's no power back there, except for the security light, so don't bother looking for a light switch – there ain't one. Dad wired a lamp on the desk directly, so you might try that if the bulb isn't burned out. Dad had a lot of stuff in a big grey file cabinet in the corner. If he had anything, that's where it'd be."

"Do you want to go out there with me?" Selma asked.

"No. It's muddy out there. My shoes – I'm in the middle of a game," Jack said. "It's okay, just go on out there and look for what you need. I don't care. There ain't nothin' out there worth stealin' anyway."

"What are you playing?" Selma asked.

"Oh! Assassin's Revenge." Jack stepped back into the darkness within the doorway. "If you find something you can use, you can keep it. It's nothing to me. Just close the barn door when you leave."

Selma could hear him walking down the hallway. She rounded the house beneath threatening skies and walked toward the big red barn. She saw a large padlock in the latch of the barn door, but it was unlocked. It hung open from the hasp. She slid the heavy rolling door sideways and peered into the darkened room. Lightning flashed, and the deep low rumble of thunder panned the sky. The perfect scene for a movie murder, she thought. It was eerie.

Shining her light around, she saw a raised platform in the left corner of the barn. A desk and chair sat in front of a wall of cardboard boxes. Selma hoped she wouldn't have to go digging through all of them. She tried the switch on the lamp and was pleased that the bulb was still good. It was not much light, but it gave her enough to turn off her flashlight. Now she could use both hands. Looking around, she saw the file cabinet Jack had mentioned. She pulled open the drawers and searched the jumble of files inside. It was a mess. There was no order to them at all. It would take weeks to go through all those folders.

Selma wiped off the seat of the leather chair and sat at the desk. *"Maybe it was one of his last cases,"* she thought as she opened the center drawer. On top of a chaotic stack, Selma found a manila folder. There was a number marked on the tab. 20161130J57. Selma pulled the case file out of her bag – the number matched! With nervous fingers, she opened the manila folder and found 8x10 glossy folders of a murdered girl. The victim was dressed as Evie Frye.

Selma stuffed both folders into her bag and switched off the lamp. She was immediately blinded by the dark, but there was enough light from the open barn door that she could see her way out. Lightning flashed outside, and the rumble of thunder grew louder. A storm was building. She wanted to get home before it got too bad. She stepped off the platform, walked toward the door, and bumped into someone in the dark. Selma yelped and stepped back as a flash of lightning revealed Jack dressed in a dark hoody and wearing fishing waders. The room went dark again.

"Did you find what you wanted?" Jack asked.

# 12

Jack found a parking place on the street near the Colorado Convention Center. It paid to arrive early. Jack put the maximum amount of change into the parking meter and got back in the van. He had attended the Denver Comic-Con before. It was a good place to get costume ideas and to photograph cosplayers. It was in Denver when he saw someone playing Evie Frye for the first time. Well, she had to be stopped, of course.

The event registration table opened at nine o'clock, so Jack donned his Batman mask and hurried to the door to register. No one was around, but The Joker was handling the sign-up table. "Sup, Batman?" he slurred around his bacon bagel.

"I need a one-day vendor pass, please."

"No can do," Joker laughed with his insane cackle. "Sold out, amigo," he smiled.

"Sold out?" Jack's heart sank.

"Should've registered early," the Joker admonished. "It's a big show. Lots of vendors."

"Are you sure? What about cancellations? Did anyone cancel?"

"Won't know until ten – check back then. I may have something for you."

"But I've got a lot of stuff. I need to load in now, before the show," Jack protested. "I can't do it while Comic-Con is going on."

The Joker checked his folder without success. He sadly shook his head. You could tell it was a put-on – he didn't care. The smile gave it away.

"Are  you sure?" Jack insisted. "Maybe someone called in this morning. Can you check?"

"All right. Hang tight. I'll see if I can help you out here. I'm not supposed to leave the desk. Can you watch it for me? I gotta go in the office back there," he pointed with his head. "I'll be back in a minute."

As soon as the Joker was out of sight, Jack moved around to the back of the table. He scanned the list of day vendors and picked one at random. He dialed the Comic-Con office number from the phone on the table.

"Denver Comic-Con," someone answered. "This is Carole. Can I help you?"

"Yeah, hey! I'm Mike Fisher, I've got booth 347, but I'm going to have to back out. I can't come today. Death in the family."

"Oh, we are so sorry, Mr. Fisher. Our condolences. We certainly understand. Please be patient for two or three weeks until we can get your refund. Normally, last-minute cancellations are not refundable, but given the circumstances, we will this time. Condolences to you and your family."

Jack came back around the table. After a few minutes, the Joker returned with a tote bag full of swag, a vendor pass on a lanyard, and the most important piece of all: A load-in/parking pass. "You're in luck! You won't believe this! Some dude called in to cancel while I was standing there talking to Carole." The Joker sat in his chair and drew out a form. "Just fill this out. How will you be paying?" he asked.

"Cash," Jack said with a smile. He filled out the form and laid two one=hundred dollar bills on the table. The Joker didn't even read the document, stamped it "PAID," and put the cash in his back pocket. That cash will never make it to the office, Jack thought.

"You're all set. Booth 347," the Joker said. "Here are the vendor rules and your passes. You can load in now, but we ask you not to load out until after the event closes today. It's only good for one day. Are you sure you don't want to stay tomorrow – it's included?" When Jack shook his head no, Joker continued, "So most vendors start breaking down around four o'clock." The Joker handed Jack the parking pass, "You'll need this to get in the back lot where the dock is. You probably ought to go ahead and get set up. We open the doors at noon today."

"Got it," Jack called back over his shoulder as he went towards the exit. "I'll do that right now."

Jack pulled off the Batman mask and placed the parking pass on the dashboard. He looked at the junk in the gift bag and found nothing there of use. Jack wasn't worried about the previous owner of booth 347. When the vendor arrived, he would flash his badge at the door and go directly to his stall as if nothing had happened. Since Jack had no intention of setting up a booth, no one would be the wiser. All Jack needed was the parking pass to the back loading dock. All of the information on Jack's registration form was fake. He was off the grid. He didn't even care if the Joker turned in the money or not. He tilted his chair back as far as it would go, put on a sleeping mask, and drifted off.

Selma pushed the photographs across the desk to Thorn. "Look at these," she said with anticipation in her voice.

Thorn took a quick look. "Yeah, what about 'em?"

"See the girl?"

"Yeah. Hannah Gleason. So what?"

"Look closer," Selma encouraged.

Thorn shook his head. "Look closer – at what?"

"That's not Hannah Gleason," Selma informed him.

"Where did you get these?" Thorn asked.

"One of Burnie's two-year-old cold case files. Look how she's dressed," Selma urged.

"Yeah, that Emmy Frye character you've been talking about."

"Evie," Selma corrected him. "Two years before Hannah, another girl died during Comic-Con dressed as the same character."

Thorn pushed the photos back to Selma, "Okay. That don't prove they are connected," he stressed. "You told me lots of people go to those things in costume."

"They do, but not many go dressed as Evie Frye. She's not like Supergirl, Wonder Woman, or Harley Quinn – many people go dressed as those characters. Hardly anyone ever goes as Evie Frye. Something about Evie Frye trips the killer off. Evie Frye is his trigger – don't you see the connection?"

"No, not really," Thorn decided. "There is one big problem. You solve that, and I'll admit you've got a legitimate lead."

"What's that?" Selma asked.

"I want you to tell me one way – just one way a maniac can snatch a young girl and abduct her in a crowded event hall without anyone noticing anything. Can you tell me that?"

"No," Selma admitted, "not yet – but there has to be a way."

"You give me a reasonable scenario, and we'll dig deeper. I'm interested," Thorn admitted. "I'm just not convinced."

"How do you think he got her out? Selma asked.

"I told you: She hooks up at the event; they go out to go necking, and something happened. Look! I'm not saying we're not dealing with a killer here. I don't think so, but crap happens. Without any marks of violence on the bodies, we've got to assume she willingly accompanied her assailant. And, we don't even know if it was a homicide. Hannah's wasn't a homicide. How did this one die?"

Selma flipped some pages in the file and looked up. "Suffocation," she said.

"Find the coroner's report, and we'll talk again," Thorn promised.

Selma searched the file and came up empty. "I'll get with the Corner's Office for a copy," Selma said as Thorn stood.

"Burney," he grumped as he left the room.


Somehow Jack knew he was dreaming, but he seemed powerless to regain consciousness. In the dream, he visualized himself as Spring-heeled Jack who had terrorized urban London for ages. Spring-heeled Jack could not be caught because of his incredible leaping ability – hence the name. Jack could leap high fences and even onto roofs without a running start. He had this dream before – many times. The dream replayed over and over in his mind like a video he had seen a thousand times.

The dark streets of 1880s London beckoned. Thick fog blanketed the city as it curled and licked through the alleys. Jack watched from the shadows as a well-dressed man stopped near the corner and lit his pipe. Jack expected the man would be at this exact spot. Late-night carriages clopped by, delivering the swells to their homes from the pubs they frequented until closing. Beneath the gaslight, the stranger leaned on his cane and smoked. He was in no hurry. The stranger did not attempt to hail the cabs that slowed expectantly as they passed him. Fog, like a spirit, floated above and around the man as he waited in the halo of light. Jack felt as one with the mist; it seemed he could hang and swing aloft without the slightest danger of being detected – like a ghost.

The well-dressed stranger was someone important, but Jack could not place him. He was not drunk or confused. He simply waited with steady resolve. In time, a couple appeared from out of the fog. Jack knew them – there was no doubt it was Evie and her brother, Jacob Frye. If he could have, Jack would have taken them out then and there. But Jack, like an inanimate spirit, seemed unable to interact in this dream world. They could not see him, but he could see and hear them quite clearly.

The stranger finally spoke, "You are late, my dears. What kept you?"

"We were … delayed," Jacob responded. "Inadvertently."

The stranger nodded, "Makes no difference. You are here now, aren't you? Tell me," he added, "are you superstitious?" he asked.

"Not particularly, Professor," Jacob responded.

"And you?" the professor turned toward Evie.

"About what?" Evie replied. "It depends."

"Wise girl, this," the professor smiled at Jacob. "You should be more attuned to her instincts," the professor laughed. "No worries. I'm skeptical about certain things. However, about other things, I am dead certain."

"Such as," Jacob inquired.

"Ghosts," the professor admitted. "I'm not skeptical about ghosts. What is odd is that I'm dead certain there are ghosts all around us. Dead certain," he repeated with a crooked smile. We live in a city that is the most advanced in the world – one with a horrendous past. Hence, the average person is so enrapt with the idea of spirits that they become easy victims of those who would use their superstition for gain. Don't you agree?"

Both twins nodded in agreement. "Indeed."

"I have an assignment for you," the professor declared. "It is not an easy assignment, and it may involve something mystical – perhaps not."

"We are intrigued," Jacob assured him.

"It may be a poor soul inhabited by a demon – you do believe in demons, don't you? Perhaps it is a demon so vile and vicious that it forces the poor sycophant it inhabits to act as it wills. Or it may be someone who is truly insane and acting of his own free, demented will. Or perhaps, it could be simply something truly evil – a filthy obscene-minded person filled with hate in his heart and ice in his veins."

"Matters not," Evie assured the professor. "Name him, and we shall do as you wish."

The professor blew grey smoke from his pipe, which quickly mingled with the swirling mist under the gas lamp. "I am speaking, of course, of an infamous, evil murderer, the butcher Jack the Ripper."

"Consider it done," Evie promised. "Consider it done."

"No!" screamed Jack, as he whirled silently around them. "Not my son!" He screamed unheard. He flailed against them harmlessly, as they could neither see nor hear his cries of anger and frustration. Gradually, the group turned and parted the swirling mist as they disappeared along the damp streets of London.

# 13

Late in the afternoon, Thorn leaned on Selma's desk. "You left these on my desk." He slid the photographs across to her.

"Thanks," Selma said, not even looking up.

Thorn stood for a moment, looking down at the pictures he had just returned. Something did not look right, but he could not quite put his finger on what looked out of place. He picked up the photos again and looked them over closely. Something was not right, and Thorn's instincts would not let it go. Suddenly, it occurred to him – no date stamp and no file numbers.

"Say! Where did you get these? They aren't logged in as evidence yet."

"Burnie's case file," Selma mentioned.

"That makes sense. Ole Burnie was not the best at keeping records. You know, one time, it got so bad he had all these records and statements just piled in the trunk of his car. We like to never sorted it all out." Thorn laughed at the memory. "I sure miss that guy, but I don't miss this kind of stuff."

"That's what I heard. Is that why Burnie was let go?"

"Let him go?" Thorn asked.

"Yeah, didn't they let him go? Because of all that stuff he did against procedures?"

Thorn looked at her and marveled at her youth. He shook his head. "It was a different time then. You could get away with a lot back then – not now, of course," he added quickly. "No, he wasn't let go. Burnie got sick and had to retire. It got so bad he had to be in a wheelchair. He had to buy a special wheelchair van to haul his ass around in." Thorn turned to walk away, still chuckling at the memory of his dead partner.

Selma looked up from her computer, "Yeah. I saw it."

Thorn stopped in his tracks. He stood still a moment before turning to face Selma. The smile was gone from his face. "What do you mean, you saw it?" he asked as he twisted his head to one side.

"I saw the van. It was in his driveway – white van with a wheelchair lift on it."

"Burnie's driveway?"

"Yeah. Burnie's driveway."

"You were at his house?"

"Yeah. I drove out there to see what I could find. There were no pictures in this case file, so after hearing all the stories about him taking stuff home, I went out to see if I could find something out there. There they are," she pointed at the pictures. "He had them in a desk in his old barn."

"You did what?"

"I went out …."

"I heard you! I just can't believe you did it. We can't use those photos now. You broke the chain of custody. They are worthless. Do not put them in that file! They will corrupt the evidence. If we ever catch the killer, the DA will never accept them."

"I realize that, but they do prove that both victims were dressed as Evie Frye."

"They don't prove any such thing! They don't even have case numbers on them, or dates, or anything else."

"The file folder they were in was marked with the case number -- 20161130J57. It matches."

"How did you even know where he lived?"

"I'm a detective," she grinned. "Besides, he had a sticky note in the file with an address on it. It turned out to be his."

"Why didn't you run this past me?" Thorn demanded.

"You were out of the country," Selma reminded him. "What was I supposed to do? Call you while you are on an airplane? I just went out there. Met his kid – he was very helpful, but kind of weird …."

"You met Jackie? How did he look? How was he?"

"Jackie? Jack, yes. He told me where to look. Scared the crap out of me in the dark, but he let me take the photos. He is very creepy," Selma added. "He was very concerned about what I had found in the barn. It was spooky with all those hooks hanging on chains from the rafters."

"Burnie was a deer hunter. He dressed his own game," Thorn said.

"I know you're right," Selma nodded, "we can't prove where those photos came from – maybe I should check up on Jackie and see what he's been up to."

"Forget that idea!" Thorn snapped. "You just put that thought out of your head right now. I've known that kid since he was five. He's no killer. Little league, Boy Scouts, Pop Warner, high school – there ain't nothing wrong with Howard's kid. Burnie was my partner for fifteen years. I'm the kid's godfather."

"He plays that game," Selma said. "Assassin's Revenge."

"So, what? You said a lot of people play that game," Thorn reminded her. "Millions."

"Yeah, but they don't have pictures of dead murder victims in their barns."

"They don't have fathers who were homicide detectives either. Let it go, Selma. Jack didn't have a thing to do with either of these cases. If he was like that, I'd know. He's just a little odd – that's all.

"He's a lot odd if you ask me," Selma insisted. "He was wearing fishing waders over his pants."

Thorn sat down before he spoke. "Selma, a cop's kid goes through a lot. He hears things – sees things that other kids don't see. They are ostracized by the other kids and called rat-finks and narcs. You don't know what these kids go through. Sometimes they see things they shouldn't see. It messes them up."

"What did Jackie see?" Selma pressed.

"He was fifteen. Howard took him out with him on a run – against the rules, of course. It was just a routine investigation – interviewing the parents of a murder victim. The kid was supposed to stay in the car. When they got to the scene where a man had shot his wife and committed suicide – it was a bloody mess. While he was calling it in, Jackie got out of the car. When his dad found him, Jackie was crouched by the dead father looking at blood splatters on the wall and floor. There was blood all brain matter over the kid's shoes. Jackie became obsessed with his shoes and his pants – they have to be immaculate. Poor kid spent a year or two in therapy. It messed him up – but he's no killer. He just can't stand to be around blood. He can't stand anything on him that looks like blood – ink, mud, coffee, chocolate – he panics."

"Oh. Yeah, that would explain a lot," Selma agreed. "Some things you can't un-see. If you don't think it's connected..."

"It's not," Thorn assured her. "You might have something on this Comic-Con thing, but just leave Jackie out of it – okay? The kid's been through enough."

"Okay, sure," Selma reassured him.

Selma was not completely convinced, but out of loyalty to Thorn, she decided to set her suspicions aside for the time being. If the kid were involved, she'd find some other tie-in down the trail. Two victims, two years apart, dressed as the same character, needed more digging. Selma pulled up the dates for all the Comic-Cons scheduled in San Antonio for the past years. No other murders on those dates came to the surface. Selma began to have doubts about the cosplay angle. Something just did not add up.

Arriving home later that night, she could hear her phone ringing inside as she unlocked her door. Throwing her purse on the couch, she rushed to pick up the phone.

"Hello."

"Selma! Is that you?" a voice asked.

"Yes. This is Selma." The voice sounded familiar. "Josh? Is that you?"

"You remembered," Josh exclaimed. "What's up, buttercup?" Josh said in his familiar greeting.

"Josh Logan! How are *you*? Man! It's been a long time. How are things up in Denver?"

Selma remembered the good times she and Josh had shared. Josh was an instructor at the police academy. Selma had a big crush on him, but they couldn't do anything about it until after she graduated. She and Josh frequently dated during her first year on the force. Selma was crushed when Josh accepted the job as a homicide detective in Denver.

"You want to come up here and find out?" he teased.

"You have a job for me? I might just do that," she laughed.

"Not right now, but maybe soon. Tonight, I just want to pick your brain."

"About what?"

"I remember you played a lot of these computer games and stuff. We even went to Comic-Con together once. Remember?"

Selma laughed, but her senses were on alert. "Comic-Con. How could I forget? You looked so ridiculous as the Joker! I still have that picture. It'll turn up at your retirement party someday," Selma teased.

"It better not! Anyway, I've got a case up here that might involve some of the Comic-Con people."

"What is it," Selma said pensively.

"We've got a 17-year old female murder victim. She was strangled in a park. Her name is Shiree Davis, and it looks like she may be dressed in a costume of some sort – like cosplay. Can you take a look and tell me which character she's supposed to be?"

Selma sat straight up in her chair. "Sure. Can you send me a picture?"

"I'm e-mailing them right now," Josh assured her.

"I'll call you back when I see it," Selma promised and hung up the phone.

Two minutes later, Selma downloaded the photo attachment and stared into the dead face of another Evie Frye.

# 14

The pictures landed with a snap as Selma dropped two photographs on Thorn's desk. "Look at these."

Thorn pushed them back with a scowl. "You showed them to me yesterday," he grumped.

"Look again. These aren't the same pictures."

Thorn sighed and looked at the crime scene pictures. "They look the same," he grunted.

"They aren't," Selma assured him. "These were taken this week."

Thorn looked up at Selma over the top of his readers. "Same girl," he offered.

"Nope," Selma assured him. "Same character – Evie Frye. Different girl."

"This week? Where?"

"Denver. At the Denver Comic-Con. Denver PD and I talked last night."

"Aw geez," Thorn grumbled, "are we on this again? I told you, you tell me how he got her out of a crowded convention center without drawing a witness, and I'll give you a little more slack."

"I still don't know that," Selma replied. "That's why I need to go to Denver," she added quickly.

"Denver? You want me to let you go to Denver? That's not gonna happen," Thorn sat back in his chair with his arms crossed. The muscles in his jaw clenched and unclenched several times.

"Why not?" Selma asked defiantly, setting her own jaw.

"Why not?" Thorn pretended to be shocked. "Because you work for us – that's why. Because it costs money to take these junkets – and besides, it's out of state. Captain won't go for it. Forget it!"

"This is fresh, Thorn. Clues are still there," she insisted.

"Let Denver PD handle it," Thorn said, waving her off. "We've got enough cases of our own."

There was a short silence as Selma weighed her next words. She turned her head but watched him out of the corner of her eyes. "That's why they called me."

"They called you?" Thorn was astonished.

"Last night. They want me to help them catch the killer. They think I'm on to something with the Comic-Con connection. At least, they want to give me a chance." Selma fought to keep the I-told-you-so tone out of her voice.

"Why you?"

"Because I know about gaming and how these characters relate to one another – that's why. At least they don't have this preconceived notion that all this is a waste of time. They are willing to listen; why aren't you?"

Thorn wrinkled his brow. "Three victims, all dressed the same way, and all during Comic-Con, right?"

Selma nodded.

Thorn put his face in his hands and slumped in his chair. He propped his chin with one hand and drew little invisible circles on his desktop. "Okay," he finally muttered. "I'll grant you that three victims seem a little more than a coincidence. It's a mystery. But why do you need to go to Denver? If I give you time to follow up on this, can't you do it by phone or by conference call or something?"

"No, Thorn, because you aren't a true believer. I understand and respect you for that. This is a hot case; in a week, it'll be a cold case. I need to be there to interview witnesses. The trail is warm, Thorn; like you said, someone has to know something. I need to be able to talk to them."

"I never said that," Thorn denied.

"You said for him to get her out of that crowded place, someone needed to see something. I need to be there to find out what they saw," Selma argued.

"I don't think I can make that work," Thorn shook his head. "I don't think the Chief will pay for that kind of investigation. It's their crime – not ours," he added.

"It is ours, too. Two of the victims are from here. Thorn, there may be more out there that we don't know about." She paused, "Is it okay with you if I go see the Captain?"

"You want to go over my head?" Thorn bristled.

"No, not unless you let me. I'll keep it between you and me; I just want a chance to explain why I need to be there."

Thorn stopped drawing circles and started tapping his forefinger on the desk. He did that when he was trying to make a decision. The silence was deafening.

"Do you trust me or not?" Selma finally asked.

"Okay, let me go talk to him. It's a long shot, but I'll give it a try – I really will. But don't be surprised if he shoots us down," Thorn relented quietly.

"If he does, can I go to him then?" Selma pressed.

"Yeah, just let me try first," Thorn agreed. "Don't worry; I'll put a good face on it."



Upstairs, Captain George Rangell was loading newly sharpened pencils into his new yellow pencil cup.

"I see you got a new pencil holder," Thorn grunted as he entered. "This one is yellow like the last one."

"Yeah, 'cause you broke the old one," the Captain groused.

"This 'uns got a smiley face on it," Thorn observed wryly.

"Yeah – Bunny's idea – she thought it would keep me in a better mood."

"Is it working?"

Rangell glared at Thorn, looking every bit like the old Marine bulldog icon, front teeth exposed and all. "What do you think?" he growled.

Thorn shook his head and sat in the visitor chair. He reached over, picked up the new pencil cup, and fiddled with it as he talked. "This ain't gonna make you much happier," he sighed.

"What have you done now?"

"Nothin'. This ain't about me. It's that girl – Detective Cibolo, I mean. She wants to go to Denver."

"Ain't happenin'," Rangell shook his head, his eyes glued to the pencil cup as if Thorn had taken his bone.

"That's what I told her, but she wants to come up here and pitch her case directly to you."

"You tell it, then – you're here." The captain crossed his arms as he listened. That's good, thought Thorn – closed arms show a closed mind – he's not going to let this happen.

"You know we've been tracking the case the last couple of months because Cibolo won't put it to sleep." Thorn passed the file to the Captain, who read it as Thorn talked. "Coroner says natural causes, but Cibolo thinks she was abducted at the Comic-Con – says the girl was dressed as a character named Frye – Evie Frye, I think it was. Anyway, she did some backtracking and found a case from a couple of years back." Thorn passed the second case file to Rangell. "This girl was strangled and was dressed in the same costume. It happened at the close of Comic-Con the year before last. Selma's convinced that some lunatic is going around killing the same character at these Comic-Cons."

"Why does she think that, and what does it have to do with Denver?" Rangell asked.

Thorn passed the newest pictures over to his boss. "This one was in Denver – last weekend."

Rangell looked from the new photos to the other ones in the files. "That's very odd," he nodded. "I can see the angle," he admitted. The captain looked up at Thorn, "Maybe, she's on to something," he mused.

"You've got to be kidding." For the second time that day, a wave of shock washed over Thorn, and he felt like his eyebrows hit the ceiling. "You're actually thinking about letting her go?" His jaw shut with an audible click as it tightened on his face.

"You don't see it?" Rangell asked. "Look. Three victims, all dressed the same way, and all killed during Comic-Cons. It's a pattern. Is it that hard to imagine that some nut case is out there whacking the same comic book character? Is this Evie character such a badass that three killers could be after her?"

With exaggerated care, Thorn gently placed the captain's yellow pencil holder back in its original position.

As Thorn walked toward the door, the Captain added, "I'll give her two weeks up there."

Thorn shook his head as he entered the hallway. "I don't even know you anymore," Thorn shot back over his shoulder as he stomped down the hall.

Rangell managed to keep the smirk off his lips until Thorn rounded the corner and was gone – but just barely.

# 15

The wind shifted off the River Thames and now blew in from landward. The sea fog wafting across the city was loaded with the putrid brown and black smoke swirling from thousands of coal-fired chimneys. Anyone out in those conditions was covered from head to foot. If you left your forearm exposed, the fog would condense on your skin in a viscid film. If you rubbed the dampness from your arm across your forehead, a glob or glutinous black slime, like brown snot, dripped downward across your lips. Entire areas of the city were posted with signs warning of health hazards. Phlegm would form deep in your throat until you coughed up black, bile-looking mucus. Masks or mufflers were useless, though indispensable to limit the quantity of soot that entered your lungs.

The eddying, churning blackness would even blot out the moon on nights like these. Only a slight halo was visible where the moon was supposed to be. It was perfect for Jack, as only those who had a pressing need would be out in the strange, choking atmosphere. Sniffing his perfumed handkerchief, Jack stepped over the open sewer that ran along the street. Jack's victims were prostitutes and dope fiends who frequented the darkened shadows. But tonight, Jack was not collecting samples for his studies. Tonight, he would try to stop those who would destroy him and expose him as the infamous Jack the Ripper. Jack could not have that happen.

Jack paused in the deep gloom of the iron-gated fence. Most people avoided this place at all costs—horrible stories circulated about the cruelty exhibited inside. The Bethlem Royal Hospital for the Criminally Insane was simply known as Bedlam Asylum by the local population. Everyone knew what it was and why it was there. It was easy to slip unseen out of the asylum – if you were the Master Surgeon. Jack could come and go as he pleased. The trick was going unseen and unobserved. Tonight, the heavy fog helped obscure his movements and was the perfect cover for a man dressed entirely in black.

Jacob Frye and his sister Evie had dogged Jack for months. Once, close friends and companions, Jack had joined the secret society of assassins. That was before Jack the Ripper became so well known. Jacob Frye had been Jack's mentor and guide. But over time, Jack became disenchanted with the idea of fighting evil. Jack wanted more. He needed to understand the role of physiology in psychiatry. Were there clues in the internal organs that predisposed certain humans to become violently insane? It was such a young science. The workings of the brain were mystical and not well understood by any. Jack believed there were bodily functions at work rather than pure mental distress. His study took him farther and farther away from his association with the group of assassins. Hostile feelings increased due to Jack's departure, and now the group of assassins feared that Jack would betray them.

Even tonight, Jacob plotted for Jack's demise. The master assassin was conspiring to eliminate his master slayer. Jack now dispatched his victims for their scientific value, not their criminal intent. Jacob feared that if the authorities caught Jack, he might reveal the existence of the gang of assassins that were slowly clearing the city of London of evildoers. Jack himself had now become one of the evil ones. In that way, Jack became the target instead of the weapon. He knew Jacob had been following him for weeks. Now, with Jacob's sister away on another case, Jack knew this was the perfect time to remove this threat to his life's work. He must permanently eliminate both Jacob and Evie.

Moving from the shadows of the hospital, Jack made his way carefully toward the docks. He knew it would not be long before Jacob followed. That was all part of Jack's plan. Jacob would assume that Jack was out "collecting samples" again and be unaware of his presence. What a stupid man. What a clumsy fool he was to think he could trick Jack so easily. Jack ambled around the streets for an hour before he knew that Jacob was behind him in the inky blackness. Jack followed an aimless strumpet through the shrouded alleys as Jacob dutifully followed, expecting Jack to make his move at every corner. Jack knew that if he attacked and downed this helpless woman, Jacob would spring from the shadows, intent on eliminating the infamous murderer from the city. Jacob could then play the hero's role – the man who stopped Jack the Ripper.

The harlot also knew she was being stalked. She slowed beneath a corner light and waited for Jack to come alongside. Drat! He had gotten careless and tipped her off too soon. Maybe he could work it for his purposes.

"Evenin', deary. Care to buy a lady a pint?" she said with a toothy smile.

"Are you quite insane?" Jack responded.

"Are you, my dear? That is the question, isn't it" she bantered.

"I'm not completely sure," Jack chuckled. Beneath the lamp, they laughed together at his joke. Jack knew that

Jacob was observing from beyond the shadows. "I may be mad and not know it," he added.

"So what about it, Luv? Are you up for a bit 'o comp'ny?"

"Not tonight, my dear. I have something much more … sinister in mind," Jack said.

Jack watched as the woman gripped a sharp stiletto beneath her shawl. "What might that be? You're not that monster that stalks the night with murderous ambition, are ya'?"

"I assure you, madam, you are quite safe from me tonight. But, I do have something for you that will not require you to lift your skirts, if you don't mind."

"Oh, yes. You're of that type, are you?" She laughed again.

Jack lowered his voice. "No, not that either, dear. You see, I'm being followed at this very moment."

"Oh, my! Is it the police?"

"No, he's not the police. But he is intent on doing me harm. Fear not!" Jack caught her arm as she turned to run away. "He is not after you, but I must know who he is. I will depart from you straight away, and he will come along shortly. Please observe him closely. Engage him as you did me. Later, I will circle back, and you can tell me of his appearance. I must be sure the right man is following."

"And you will pay me for this information?"

"Of course – and perhaps a little extra, too, if you get his name."

"Consider it done, m'luv."

"If he asks you why I passed you by, you can tell him I promised to return shortly. Do you understand that?"

"Indeedy. You will be back?" She asked.

"With your payment," Jack promised.

"Perhaps I can get paid by him too?"

"If that suits you well," Jack answered. "However, do not stray far from this area. I will find you," Jack whispered as he disappeared into the gloom.

Jack was back on the same street within three-quarters of an hour, but he did not see the woman. Perhaps she had ducked into the nearby alley. In the filthy passageway between streets, he found her. Jack could barely see a body indecently splayed on her back. She reclined motionless in a pool of bloody pavement. Blood splattered the wall next to the obscene body, and Jack knew from experience she was quite dead. Bloody poor work, he thought as he examined the woman.

"Did I pose her quite properly?" a voice spoke from the darkness.

Jack whirled about and finally detected the dim shape of Jacob in the darkness. "I know you have your standards, Jack, dear boy. I did not want to confuse the authorities as to who committed this grisly offense. It appears you have bagged another one, old chum."

"Yes, quite," Jack mumbled, "so it does appear." Unseen by Jacob in the darkness, Jack pulled the chloroform bottle wrapped in cloth from his pocket. He removed the top as he pretended to examine the body, knowing that Jacob would rush him while he was distracted. Dashing the chemical onto the cloth, Jack was ready as Jacob ran from the shadows. Jack swung his cane to fend off Jacob's knife. Reversing the rod and using it as a club, Jack surprised Jacob with a powerful blow to the forehead. Overpowering the smaller man, Jack placed the cloth across his face. In seconds, Jacob was unconscious.

Placing his arm around the fallen man's back and under his armpit, Jack drug the unconscious Jacob toward the street. He leaned the body against a lamppost. In a few moments, Jack could hear the clopping hoof beats of an approaching carriage.

"Can you help us, mate?" Jack called as he flagged down the passing lorry. Jack imitated his best cockney, "Me mate 'as 'ad a bit too much cheer, I'm sure. Can ya take us to our quarters?"

"You'll have to load 'im yerself, then lad. Where to? Moreover, ye'll 'ave to pay fer two besides, even though he won't get the enjoyment of it."

Lifting Jacob into the bed of the carriage, Jack gave the driver the address.

"Why, that be Bedlam Asylum, mate. Are ya' quite sure?"

"Yes. This man is an escaped inmate. Get us there quickly before he recovers his senses."

"Gid'up!" the driver called his horse as it dashed off in a gallop.

Jack half-dragged, half-carried Jacob into the darkness behind the hospital to a back entrance reserved for staff. "We have a new admittance, dear," he told the matron who unlatched the door.

"Shall we take him upstairs, Doctor?" she asked.

"No, nurse. This is a special case. I shall take him to a holding room in the basement until I can examine him further. He may be dangerous for all I know. Once he is awake, I shall interview him thoroughly. Mind, my dear, make no note in the record as he might be just a harmless drunkard. If needed, and he requires admittance, I will register him in the morning. Meanwhile, we shall let him sleep it off, shall we?"

"Yes, Doctor."

After dismissing the night nurse, Jack lugged the comatose Jacob down the stone steps into the darkened bowels of the insane asylum. It was where they kept the worst of them. It was a place where no one knew or cared who was held there. It was the perfect place to hide Jacob Frye until his meddlesome sister came calling. Jack knew she would. Jack also knew that he would have them both right where he wanted them when she arrived – quite dead.


Jack woke in the darkness laughing hysterically. For a moment, he was disoriented and unsure of where he was. Gradually he realized he was in his bedroom outside San Diego. He must get busy. Comic-Con in Orlando was only a week away. He must prepare.

# 16

Selma climbed the jetway toward the arrival gate at Denver International. She wondered if things would be uncomfortable with Josh after being separated for a year. Selma didn't know if what she had for Josh was love or not; she just knew she felt happy whenever he was around. She realized she had not been really happy since he left. Selma knew he would be standing at the arrival gate waiting for her to come through the door and wondered if the greeting would be awkward. She felt her face flush as she neared the top of the sky bridge. Had he met someone else? Would it be different? She need not have worried.

Josh grabbed her and planted a kiss right on her lips almost as soon as she entered the waiting room. Suddenly, all Selma's doubts evaporated in Josh's tight embrace. Things had not changed.

"Wow!" she blinked a few times for dramatic effect. "That was some welcome. Do you greet all of your visiting detectives this way?" Selma laughed.

"Only you," Josh blushed a little. "Man, am I glad to see you. I can't believe you're here. I've missed you so much," he gushed.

"Well, you could have called," she teased.

"Ah, you know … I was gone. I didn't want to get in your way or anything. I was afraid you may have moved on – you know? Maybe there was someone else …" his voice trailed off into embarrassed silence.

"What if there was? You may have just kissed someone's wife, Mr. Logan. Did you ever think of that?"

"Did I?" A worried look crossed his face. "Are you? I mean  -- I was just so happy to see you – I didn't think there might be – I'm sorry."

He looked so pitiful Selma let him off the hook. "Don't worry," she punched him in the chest. "I'm still single, you dope. Don't you even look at my social media page? Come on. Let's get out of here."

Once in the car, Josh headed toward the downtown area. "You are getting the VIP consultant treatment. The Department put you up at the Coloradan. It's central to downtown and not far from the station. I've been given the privilege of shepherding you around. You ever been to Denver before?"

"No, I haven't. I'm glad we'll be working together. I've missed you," Selma admitted.

"I'm just shocked they let you come. How did you ever talk Rangell into this? He's normally as tight as a bass drum."

"I didn't – Thorn did," Selma admitted.

"Thorn Nix?" Josh laughed. "He's worse. You must be something really special in the Alamo City to have that kind of clout," Josh kidded. "But then, not everyone passes the detective exam in two years, do they?"

"I had a good teacher," Selma smiled. "What have you found out?"

"Her name was Shiree Ward. She spells it S-h-i-r-e-e. She's Caucasian, 16, and a local. Her parents are devastated, of course. I've got photos – she was a beautiful little girl." Josh passed a folder to Selma.

"What have you done so far?" Selma asked as she thumbed through the file.

"Nothing yet – we were waiting for you. We've interviewed the parents, but none of her friends yet. It's been quite a shock for everyone – it's made all the papers and TV news. They even had a picture of you on TV last night."

"A picture of me? How did they get that?"

"File photo from San Antonio, I guess. Like I said, we waited – we thought you might know the best way to proceed since you've had a couple of these cases already."

"She went there with friends and just disappeared? How odd. I see a list of names here. Have any of them been checked out?"

"Not yet," Josh admitted.

"I want to get started right away   tonight, while the trail is warm. I want to talk to those kids that were with her."

"Okay – we'll drop your bags at your room, and we'll head out. I'll make some phone calls while I wait in the lobby, okay?"

"Nonsense, come up to the room. I'll change into something, and we can leave from there. Maybe we can have dinner tonight?"

"I insist," Josh grinned. "Still like enchiladas?"

"Colorado enchiladas?" Selma looked doubtful. "Really?"

"I know – I know. You come from enchilada heaven, but they do a pretty good job up here. They're tasty."

"We'll see," Selma joked as they entered the lobby. "See if we can go see that first girl on the list – that Kendra. She was listed as a best friend."

"You got it," Josh agreed.

Kendra Lane lived in an upscale neighborhood on the northeast side near Shiree's house. The two girls were close friends, and her parents agreed to let Selma and Josh come by to talk with Kendra.

"Kendra is very upset," her mother said as she led the two detectives into the living room. "We kept her out of school again today. We thought maybe she wasn't ready to face the kids at school. Someone from the police might be interested in talking to her. Please make yourself comfortable. I'll go get Kendra – she's in her room."

In a few moments, a visibly distraught teenaged girl entered. After introductions, she sat on a nearby chair and smoothed the dress in her lap.

Selma took the lead. "Kendra, I'm so sorry for the loss of your friend, Shiree. Can you tell us what you know?"

"I'll try. I wasn't there with her; maybe if I was, this might not have happened." Tears streamed down the young girl's face.

"Kendra, you can't think that way," her mother interjected. "If you had been there, it might have happened to you too. Thank God you weren't," the mother sighed.

"Kendra," Selma said, in as soothing a voice as possible, "why weren't you there on Saturday when Shiree went?"

"We had a family reunion," the mother answered instead of Kendra. "It's an annual thing, so it was an important family event – you understand? Kendra went on Sunday, but Shiree was not there."

"Yes, ma'am," Selma nodded. "Please, Mrs. Lane, we'd like to get Kendra's story if you don't mind."

"Sure – sure. Sorry, I know I'm a little protective; and Kendra is very upset."

"I'll be gentle," Selma promised. "Kendra, tell me about Shiree's plans to go to Comic-Con."

"I was with her the night she decided on her costume," Kendra said in a soft voice. "She wanted to go as someone different than all the others. She said there would be a hundred Wonder Women, but Shiree wanted to do something different. We looked through a lot of magazines and websites until she found what she wanted."

"What did she choose."

"A character from a game – I think her name was Evie Frye."

"What game was it," Selma asked, already knowing the answer but trying to get Kendra comfortable talking.

"It was a game called Assassin's Revenge."

"Do you play that game?"

"No, ma'am. Neither did Shiree before that night. She said she was researching the character, and she played the game a few times to get to know her. That's all I know."

"Why didn't Shiree wait to go with you on Sunday?"

"She was gonna meet me there on Sunday, too. She was all excited about Saturday, though – she couldn't miss Saturday."

"Why Saturday?"

"It was something about a video – she was so excited. She said she was going to be in a video about an upcoming movie. They told her that her costume was perfect for the role. She said she was going to meet the film crew there at Comic-Con on Saturday. I thought she was just making it up, though. It didn't sound real."

"Why not?" Selma pressed.

"I don't know," Kendra shook her head. "It just sounded like it was too fantastic to be real. I mean – she never acted before, and they picked her out of the blue to appear in some video? Without anyone even seeing her act? It didn't sound right."

"How do you know they didn't see her picture?"

"Shiree's mom was strict about that. Once she sent her photo to someone on the internet, her mother restricted her internet for a month. She wouldn't make that mistake again. We talked about it. I don't send my pictures out either unless I know who is on the other end. Right, mom?"

"Absolutely. Those people out there these days – you can't trust them."

"Yes, ma'am," Selma agreed. Selma turned back toward Kendra.

"Kendra, how did she meet these people that were going to do the video?"

"I don't know," Kendra admitted.

"Did she say who they might be?"

"Not really – she wanted it to be a surprise. She told me it was someone famous who played in the movies – but she didn't say who it was. She said she would tell me all about it Sunday." Kendra's eyes clouded again, "But Sunday, she didn't show up. All we heard was that she was missing. Then, the news the next day that …."

Kendra placed her hands over her eyes and cried heavy sobs. Josh and Selma stood and thanked her mother for letting them in. As Selma passed Kendra's chair, she paused and put her hand on the girl's heaving shoulder.

"Kendra, I'm so sorry. None of this is your fault. We're going to find out who did this. We're searching through her computer and cell phone to learn who was in contact with her. We're going to do the best we can to get to the bottom of it. Whoever did this will pay. I've come all the way from Texas to try to find them," Selma promised.

"I know. I saw you on TV last night. You must be very important to come all that way," the weeping girl said.

The next name on the list was a boy named Mitch Wagner, also 17. Mitch's parents were not home, so he would not let them in. After showing their badges, Mitch agreed to talk to them from behind the screen door.

"Mitch," Selma began. "We're here to talk about Shiree Lane. I believe you know her?"

"I sure do. We had several classes together in high school. It's a shame what happened – she was a good girl."

"Were you at the Comic-Con with her?"

"Yeah, I was – a bunch of us were. Shiree was in a film or video or something the last time I saw her."

"Tell me about that," Selma encouraged.

"Man, what a rip-off! That dude – that Jack guy? He was some kind of nut case – you know? He cheated us, man – he just flat out took off and left us hanging."

"Tell me from the start," Selma said, taking a recorder out of her pocket. "Do you mind if we record this?"

"Sure – no problem. Anyway, we got to Comic-Con, and Shiree was already there. It was about an hour before closing, and she was just sitting in the snack bar area, just sitting there all by herself. So we sat down with her and started talking. That's when she told us about the video. She said they were filming a movie trailer or something, and she was going to be in it."

"Who was going to film her?"

"This guy – this Hollywood guy. He's like the stunt double for Batman and a bunch of other superheroes – you know? She was supposed to meet him there, and she was waiting for him."

"Keep going," Selma urged him.

"Well, he shows up in this costume that looked right out of Jack the Ripper, man. I mean, it was weird, so he walks up to Shiree and puts his arm around her – like he knew her for a long time. He said they would film a video about an upcoming Batman movie and that Shiree would be a key player. We were blown away, man. It was so dope! We thought she had made it up – but this was real! He said we could all be in it as extras. Then, he started giving orders."

"What kind of orders?"

"Like where to stand and what to do once the filming started. He pointed out some guys in the crowd with cameras and waved at them. Next, he went over the scene. A crowd was starting to gather, but he didn't seem to care. He said we could watch, but we'd have to not get in the way. Security came by, and he talked to them for a few minutes, and they eventually shrugged their shoulders and went away. Then, this Jack the Ripper character went away for about ten minutes and said he'd be right back. He said when he came back; the filming would have already started. He told us just to act natural."

"What was the scene?" Selma asked.

"He said he would be coming back as this character – Jack something."

"Jack the Ripper?"

"Naw – Jack spring heels or something like that. He was playing the villain, and he was going to kidnap Shiree – who was playing Evie Frye or something like that. Anyway, his costume was spot on, man. It was high-quality Hollywood stuff – not those cheap rip-offs from the costume shop. This was movie-quality stuff; you know what I'm sayin'? So, we all believed him."

"Spring-heeled Jack?" Selma asked.

"Yeah! That's his name," Mitch said.

"What happened next?"

"He was going to pretend to give her something to knock her out. Then, he was going to put her in a wheelchair and roll her out the loading dock to a wheelchair van. The cameras would be filming the whole thing, and we needed to be careful not to block the shot. He said they were going to shoot the rest of the film over at Skyline Park, about four blocks away. They had a movie set all arranged, and Batman would be there – not the movie star, but a stunt double. Batman was going to jump out of a helicopter, beat this Jack character up, and save Shiree. If we wanted to go over there, we could watch; but we had to be real quiet over there and not tell anyone else about it. They didn't want a big crowd over there."

"Out of a helicopter?"

"Well, he said they would dub that helicopter in later. Movie magic, you know? For now, it was just a scaffold Batman would swing down from – but it would look good in the movie."

Selma made eye contact with Josh before looking back at Mitch. "Are you kidding me?" she asked Mitch.

"No, ma'am. When he came back, he was pushing a wheelchair. He pulled this movie clapper thing from under his cape and showed it to the camera guys – like they do in the movies. They didn't have real movie cameras like you would think. This Jack guy said they were using HD technology, and the smaller cameras were more mobile for this type of filming. He clapped that board really loud and yelled 'Action!' Then, he pulled a white handkerchief out of his pocket, came up behind Shiree, and placed it over her mouth. I didn't know she was such a good actress, man. We were all impressed. She played the part perfectly. She slumped down into the chair, and he pushed her toward the loading docks. Heck, we even cleared the crowd out so they could get through."

"What happened then?"

"The guys with the cameras were real cool – they were professionals. If you didn't know it, you'd never know they were filming a movie. It was so great. This Jack guy loads her up in the wheelchair van and takes off. We ran through Comic-Con, out the front door, and all the way to Skyline Park."

"Yeah," Selma said. "What did you see?"

"Nothin'! Not a damned thing. There were no film trucks, or cameras, or crew, or anything like that at Skyline Park. We thought maybe he meant Creek Front Park, so we ran all the way over there – for nothing. We didn't see anything that looked like a movie set or no scaffold or anything. It was a total bust. Jimmy said they probably just told us that to get us out of the way. What a bust. We missed the whole damned thing."

"Did you see Shiree after that?"

"No, ma'am. We figured she was still acting, and they were still filming on the set – wherever that was. It wasn't until the next day we heard she was missing."

"Do you recall anything about the movie crew that might help us?"

"The guy was a movie guy, alright. He was a star at the Comic-Con, too," Mitch said as he reached for a paper on the coffee table. "Here. This is a flyer telling all about him. He's a stunt double for Batman. His father is a famous actor too – you know. Bob Russell? That's his dad!"

"Bob Russell – the movie star?"

"Yeah! That's him, man! This was his son. That's how we knew it was real. You've seen him in all the Batman movies – he's just not famous like his dad. He's Buck Russell! That's the guy that drove off with Shiree!"

Selma sucked in her breath as she turned to Josh. "That's how he gets them out!"

# 17

Selma came out of the shower and sat on her bed in her robe as she applied makeup. She flipped channels to catch the news as she dressed. Selma was anxious to see if anyone had interviewed Buck Russell yet. She knew DPD had notified Federal authorities about what she and Josh had uncovered, and she was quite sure the ball was rolling toward finding out what the suspect knew. The local news had nothing about an arrest, but she was shocked at what she heard when she switched to the national news network.

"In a pre-dawn raid this morning, federal agents, along with local Los Angeles authorities, surrounded the home of Hollywood stunt actor Buck Russell. Buck Russell is the son of Academy Award-winning actor Bob Russell. The cause of the raid is unknown at this time; however, Mr. Russell has just returned from a personal appearance in Denver. Unverified sources say that this investigation is connected to the disappearance of a young woman in Denver. Our sources say that Mr. Russell was the last person to have been seen with her."

Selma opened the door to Josh's knock. She pointed to the TV as he came into the room. "Look. They raided his house in LA. We need to go out there. I want to see him – interview him."

"We can ask," Josh agreed. "But first, we have an appointment with Ricky Weathers, the director of Denver Comic-Con. He's waiting for us."

Selma dressed quickly. Grabbing her things, she left the room with the TV playing dramatic scenes of helicopters circling Buck Russell's house. In the hallway, Selma's cell phone began ringing.

"Hello," she answered as she headed toward the elevators.

"Is this Detective Cibolo?"

"Yes, it is. Who's calling, please?"

"My name is Officer Wilbert Johnson of the New River PD in Arizona."

"Yes, sir, Officer Johnson. How can I help you?"

"I got your name and number from the Denver PD this morning after I saw the story about Buck Russell," he said. "They said you are in charge of the case there in Denver. I hope I haven't called at a bad time."

"I was just on the way out, but hold on a minute." Selma sat on the couch in the hallway outside the elevator and motioned Josh to wait. "What's going on?" she asked.

"Well, I pulled this guy, Buck Russell, over Thursday night – liked to scared hell out me!"

"Wait! You pulled Buck Russell over in Arizona before the Denver Comic-Con?"

"I sure did. I just wanted to let you know…."

"Hold on. Where is New River?"

"We are in southern Arizona, just north of Phoenix."

"You pulled Buck Russell over in southern Arizona the night before he was to appear in Denver?"

"That's what he said. He said he was headed to Denver. He even gave me an autographed picture for my kid."

"What was he doing in southern Arizona? That's hours away from the direct route from LA to Denver."

"Well, that's what I said. He said he stopped in Phoenix to see a girlfriend, and now he was headed north. He seemed to be in a hurry."

"What was the purpose of the traffic stop?"

"It was minor – just routine. It's unusual for someone out of state to be out that early around here. His license plate light was out. It gave me probable cause to pull him over and check it out – lots of drug traffic goes through here at night. He was driving a white van with a wheelchair lift installed on the side. He fixed the bulb on the scene and went on his way. I just thought you might want to know."

"I sure do. Do you have the tag number?"

"Yeah, I wrote in in my book. Since the light was repaired, I didn't issue a citation or a warning, but I wrote down the license number – well, it wasn't a number exactly – it was one of those California vanity plates that said STNTMAN. He said he did movie stunts for Batman."

Selma pulled the phone away from her ear and motioned Josh. "Check California plates STNTMAN," she said before returning to the phone.

"Officer Johnson, you told me he scared you. Can you tell me why?"

"You know how it feels when you pull someone over before dawn, and you get that funny feeling in your gut? Well, I had that feeling. I'm pretty sure the guy was packing, but he said he wasn't. Anyway, I didn't actually see anything, and I didn't want to search him for such a minor stop. Besides, he was acting decent and very cooperative. But still, I kept a close eye on him."

"Did you call for backup?"

"We're a small town, Detective. We don't have no backup. I'm the only cop on duty at that time. I'd have had to wake up the Chief, and I didn't think it was worth it. Besides, as I said, he was very compliant. Then I saw something that made my skin crawl."

"Like what?"

"Well, when he opened the back of his van, there were, like, bodies stacked one on top of another back there. At first, it looked like dead bodies piled back there! I put him up against the car – he's lucky I didn't shoot him. Turned out they were manikins."

"Manikins? What was he doing with manikins?"

"Well, when he explained, it sounded okay. He was going to this Comic-Con thing in Denver, and the dummies were all decked out in comic book hero costumes. One was even Batman. He said he was a stuntman for Batman."

Selma was scribbling away in her notebook as Johnson continued, "He told me he sets these things up at the conventions as some sort of static display."

"I see, then what?"

"Well, he fixed his plate light and went on his way. I didn't see any reason to hold him. He signed that picture, and then he drove away. I gave it to my son."

"You saw him sign it?"

"Yes, ma'am."

"Officer Johnson, that photo is evidence. Would you please mark it appropriately and overnight it  to me at the Denver PD?"

"You bet," he agreed. "I figured you'd want it."

"Well, thank you for the call. You've been very helpful, but I've got to run. I appreciate you reporting this to us."

"You bet. Hey! One more thing," Johnson added. "The news said he abducted a girl there in Denver."

"Yeah?"

"Question is – where did he put her? There ain't no way he could have stashed her with those dummies in the back, and with all that wheelchair equipment– especially if she was fighting him off."

"Unless she was **in** the wheelchair," Selma agreed and ended the call.

"California plate comes back to Buck Russell in LA," Josh told her as he held the elevator door open.

"We've got him," Selma smiled jubilantly as she pushed the button for the ground floor.

Ricky Weathers' office was on the upper floors of a bank building not far from the Colorado Convention Center. He was waiting in his office as they entered. The sign on the door read Fair Weather Promotions.

"Hi, guys," he motioned them in. "Have a seat. Have a seat. Can I offer you something? Cold water? Soda?"

Selma asked for water, and she watched as Weathers took a bottle from a small refrigerator behind his desk. "Nice view of the city and mountains," she admired.

"Thanks. We've been here for ten years. We love the place. We promote a lot of events around Denver and out at Red Rocks – music mostly. We just finished a big Comic-Con here in town."

"That's why we're here, Mr. Weathers. We want to get some information about a commercial video filmed during the event. We'll need some facts and figures."

"Commercial video? There were no film crews at our Comic-Con – if there were, I would have known it. We had some photographers going around taking candid still shots, but no videos – especially not the professional kind. I can assure you that," he stressed.

"How do you know?" Selma asked.

"Believe me; we would know. All media, including local television, have to register and get a special pass. We own the rights to all of the images taken. We have young people here; some dressed very provocatively, so we have to get a photographic model release for every official image. We're very strict about that," he assured Selma.

"There was no professional film crew here that day, TV or otherwise."

"Shiree, the missing teenager, told her friends she was in a video – some of her friends back that claim up," Selma informed him.

"Look, if some kids got together to shoot their own little streaming video, we might not know about that. But I promise you it wasn't a commercial shoot."

"They even said some of your security people stopped to talk to them as they were filming. Do you know anything about that?"

"Nope. Security may have questioned them about what was going on, but as I said, if it was an amateur group filming their friends, security would not have bothered them. It happens all the time."

"Except this time, an innocent girl was murdered," Selma reminded him.

"Of course," Weathers nodded. "What a tragic thing to happen. But – I have to say about that – you guys are on the wrong trail."

"What do you mean, sir?" Selma asked.

"Buck – Buck Russell. You guys went after the wrong man," Weathers laughed.

"He was questioned this morning in LA," Selma told him.

"Yeah, I saw that – on national TV at that! Buck Russell and his old man, Bob, are going to have your butts.

Defamation of character, slander, false arrest – you name it."

"Mr. Weathers, we're trying to solve a murder case. He's not arrested – he is what we call a 'person of interest right now. So far as I know, he has not been charged with anything."

"Well, you better hope he isn't. It's bad enough already with national news and helicopters circling his house – armed swat teams at his door. What's going to be of interest is to see how you get out of this one," Weathers grinned.

"We think we have a case, Mr. Weathers. Why do you think we don't?"

"Because he didn't do it – I know that for a fact," Weathers insisted.

"How can you possibly know that?" Selma asked.

"Because," Weathers took a long sip from his water bottle before bringing it down, "I picked him up at the airport Saturday morning at 9:00 a.m. He worked his booth at the Comic-Con until two o'clock. We had a nice lunch brought in, which we ate together. Then, I drove him over to the airport at three. He was on a plane somewhere over Utah by four in the afternoon. I was with him the entire time he was in Denver. He didn't have a girl with him."

"Was he flying in his own plane?"

"Nope, he was flyin' commercial. You can check the airlines – direct shot into LAX. He was by himself."

# 18

Back in the car, Selma was upset. "We were so close," Selma moaned. "We were so sure it was Buck Russell. Oh, my God! They surrounded Buck's house, Josh."

"I know."

"He's innocent – someone else is pretending to be Buck Russell."

"Someone is pretending to be Buck Russell, pretending to shoot Hollywood videos, and pretending to be a Comic-Con character – but which one?"

"Spring-heeled Jack," Selma said. "Spring-heeled Jack."

"Who is Spring-heeled Jack?"

"These video games," Selma explained, "are based on real events a lot of the times. That's why they seem so real. They use these old folktales to keep from having to write a lot of backstories, I guess. The real Spring-heeled Jack lived in Victorian London in the mid-eighteen hundreds. There are actual news reports of sightings. Legend has it that he was able to leap tall buildings and evaporate into thin air. He attacked women on the street and scared the hell out of them. Fear swept through town for years about Spring-heeled Jack. No one could catch him."

"What happened?"

"That's where legend and these newer versions part ways. The real Spring-heeled Jack eventually just disappeared – maybe he got too old or something. The attacks eventually stopped, and everyone forgot about him – except for the legend. Think about it, Josh – a dark, mysterious stranger is stalking in the night, dropping down from the darkness like a humongous bat. Does that remind you of someone?"

"Yeah, Batman," Josh agreed.

"Yeah, there's that. These legends spawned many stories and tales about heroes and villains who could do super-human feats. Superman, Wonder Woman, Green Lantern – those were the good ones. One, in particular, seems to stand out -- Batman."

"They do? But Batman doesn't kill people – does he? And our killer doesn't wear a Batman costume. How does that all add up?"

"I played these games a lot. You've probably read the comic books that have been coming out since the end of the 1930s. Almost every one of them has some sort of power or skill that makes them special. No, he doesn't kill people – he just brings them to justice. All the superhero characters blend together with traits from these Victorian legends and folktales."

"That makes sense."

"So, if you were immersed in these stories, you might be convinced that you could have some of the same powers. Don't you see? I believe our killer does – I think he believes he is Spring-heeled Jack, reincarnated and out for revenge."

"Is he that nuts?"

"Yeah," Selma agreed. "Okay, we've got him crossing Arizona, way out of the way from a direct route from LA. Why? Girlfriend in Phoenix? Maybe – maybe not. He's from somewhere in southern California – farther south than LA – San Diego, maybe. He travels at night in a white van marked STNTMAN. He attracts these girls by promising to use them in a movie. There is no movie. The camera operators he pointed out are probably not even in on the deal – lots of people take pictures at Comic-Con. This person is acting alone and using fantasies of stardom against these young girls. Everyone wants to be a video star these days."

"Lots of them do. Some of them have accumulated thousands of hits on their videos."

"So, where is the next major Comic-Con? He's probably on the way there right now."

Josh checked his notes. "Orlando," he said.

"We've got to get to Orlando," Selma said. See if you can get it authorized. I'll work on my end."

Selma's cell phone interrupted their planning. "It's Thorn," she told Josh before answering. Selma sat on a bench outside the police headquarters as Josh went inside.

"Detective Cibolo," Thorn said when she answered. In the background, she could hear Thorn already tapping his fingers on the desk. "I had a partner named Cibolo once," Thorn began as if telling a story. "She don't call – she don't write – she don't send flowers."

"We've been busy, Thorn, chasing down the bad guys."

"So I heard. Federal agents? Swat team in LA? Hollywood movie stars? I'll say you've been damned busy."

"Thorn, that wasn't us. We just reported what we uncovered. We had eyewitness reports of Buck Russell luring this girl out of the building. We filed the reports, and the feds picked up on it. It was an interstate trafficking team. We swung and missed, but it's only strike one."

"Strike one? It's a hell of a black eye – that's what it was. Almost a knockout punch."

"Almost?" Selma asked, hoping she wasn't being recalled to San Antonio.

"Well, you're down for the eight-count – that's for sure. They're thinking about calling you back to San Antonio."

"No, Thorn, we're close – really close. We know how he does it now. We know his motive. We know who his next victim will be. We are closing in. In two weeks, in Orlando, we'll have him for sure."

"Orlando? Now you want to go to Orlando?"

"Yes, sir," Selma said firmly.

"So you've got a guy pretending to be a movie star who is pretending to be a comic book character? Who are you going to arrest in Orlando? Mickey Mouse?" She could hear Thorn laughing.

"Damn it! That's not fair, Thorn! That's ridiculous. I see you haven't changed a bit. You still think this is a big joke. I need to go to Orlando to catch a real killer."

"I'm sorry, Selma. I was just kidding around – I couldn't resist – it's funny! Lighten up. Look, you've done your best. Why can't you just turn it over to Denver and come back here? There are other cases, you know."

"I can't, Thorn. We've come this far. We know his license plate number, and we know what kind of van he drives. He might get stopped before he even gets there. You said if I figured out how he gets them out of the building, you'd give me a longer rope."

"I know, I said that – didn't I?" Thorn admitted.

"Look," Selma explained. "We know how he does it now. We know who he's after. We're going to tail potential victims and catch him in the act. I need to be there to do that. This is the last one, Thorn. After Orlando, I'll be home whether we catch him or not – okay? I just need a little more rope."

"Yeah, like I believe that. I know you, Selma Cibolo. That's why I need you back here. You don't give up. I'll see what the Captain says – I hope it's not enough rope to hang you."


Buck Russell's arrest troubled Jack. Though it was not unexpected, the news did catch him by surprise. He knew, eventually, someone would pick up that trail. Some smart cop somewhere had fingered Buck Russell as the killer. Jack knew he could not pretend to be Buck Russell any longer. He had contingency plans, of course. It was no problem. He had planned for this possibility. He had several aliases he could use. He simply switched to a different identity. There was just enough time for him to steal another identity before going to Orlando. Several months earlier, he had selected one. It was a wicked pleasure to choose the surname of the producer of the Batman movies – Burton. Jack Burton had a nice ring to it. He had all of the documents he needed to become Jack Burton. After shuttering his home in San Diego, he drove overnight to west Texas. There, he rented a small apartment, purchased new insurance on his van in Jack Burton's name, and got a Texas auto inspection – all with cash. It did not pay to leave a credit card trail.

It was a quiet June morning in the small town of Marfa, Texas. Flowers bloomed along the sidewalk leading to the courthouse steps. The wet streets and sidewalks smelled fresh from the spring rain that had fallen earlier. Mockingbirds flitted between the two live oak trees on the shady front lawn. Unlike most courthouses, there were no front steps, just a high threshold before the large front door. Inside, a sign indicated the way toward the Tax Office.

Jack pulled a small number from the dispenser and waited for his turn. When a clerk called his number, he went to the desk.

"Hi!" he greeted the server. He looked at her nametag. People love it when you use their names. "Wilma, I just moved here from California. I bought this car in LA before leaving town, and I need to register it with Texas plates. Here is the title, signed over to me. Here are my license and insurance papers."

The woman examined his paperwork carefully. "What is your current address?" she asked.

Jack pretended to check his notes. "1723 West Palm," Jack reported as she wrote it on a pad.

"You'll need to change your driver's license to a Texas license with your current address. I'll register you and give you Texas tags, but you have thirty days to make those changes. Just wait right here."

Miss personality moved behind her desk and typed into her computer. Jack sat back on the bench and waited.

"Mr. Burton," a voice called. Wilma called twice before Jack realized she was calling for him. "Mr. Jack Burton."

"Yes, ma'am," Jack sprang to the counter.

"Mr. Burton, we have a slight problem here. This address, 1723, comes back to a vacant lot. This is a small county – we keep the property tax records here, too. There is no house at that address."

"Vacant lot? Let me see that," Jack examined the paperwork. "Oh, I see the error on the insurance form. They must have copied it wrong. My address is 1728 – not 1723. It's hard to tell a three from an eight sometimes. I'll get that fixed. I just moved in."

Wilma looked Jack directly in the eyes. She did not blink. It was only a couple of seconds, but it felt like a long time. "You have to get that fixed. I see from your California driver's license the name is correct. Was that your former address?"

"Yes, I just moved to Texas this week," he said, avoiding answering the question.

Wilma looked doubtful for a moment. After a moment, she said, "Okay, so I'm going to issue the tags. Your inspection is current, the VIN matches up, and we have your local address straightened out. But I need you to come back with a corrected certificate of insurance and a new Texas driver's license."

"Yes, ma'am, I'll be sure to do that," Jack promised. "You can count on it."

"I'm not kidding," she warned sternly. "You be back here within thirty days, or we'll revoke your tags and put out a warrant. We don't play games here in Texas."

"Ma'am," Jack said sincerely, "nothing short of death will stop me."

# 19

A yellow sun gradually rose over the muddled waters of the Gulf of Mexico. Jack realized he would have to pull over soon to wait until nightfall. Biloxi was still some eight hours away from Orlando. He guided his van to a shady spot near the Pascagoula Bridge and parked beneath a tree. Several early morning anglers parked there, so Jack knew his van would not seem out of place.

He ate his small dinner, pulled his shades, and settled in to sleep through the day. He knew better than use his Buck Russell cover, so he stayed off the computer and away from the games. Once he got to Orlando, he would buy a ticket and search for Evie. There was always an Evie. Maybe this time, he would find the real Evie – the one that would satisfy him forever.

"We're so close – I can almost feel it," Selma told Josh as they settled into their seats for the flight to Orlando.

"I know," Josh agreed. "I wonder why he needs all of those manikins," Josh wondered. "He told the Arizona cop that the manikins were used as display items at the Comic-Con, but we know he doesn't. Why does he need to haul them around with him then?"

"I know; it's strange," she agreed. "Seems like a lot of effort. He doesn't use them for displays at Comic-Cons."

"Maybe he changes costumes at different shows," Josh suggested.

"I don't think so. That would destroy the illusion. I'm pretty sure he always dresses as Spring-heeled Jack. That's his fantasy."

"Tell me again. Who was Spring-heeled Jack – and why do you think he was after Evie Frye for revenge?"

"It's a long story," Selma said.

"We've got a couple of hours," Josh assured her as he settled back into his airline seat.

Selma continued her story, mostly to work it out in her mind. She was grateful that someone was willing to listen.

"This is all theory, but this is what I've figured out from playing the game and doing some research on the internet. As I explained earlier, Spring-heeled Jack was a real character in Victorian England. People actually thought he was real. A man would jump out at women in the dark and scare them half to death. The newspapers at the time recorded the reports. It shook up his victims so badly that some of them ended up with mental problems. The mayor even conducted a kind of town hall meeting about the attacks, and the citizens were outraged."

"For real? Did that really happen?" Josh questioned.

"It sure did – it's documented in the newspapers of the time. Gradually, the attacks stopped, but no one ever caught Spring-heeled Jack. He had this amazing leaping ability. He could leap tall fences and to the roofs of buildings and get away."

"How does that tie in with Evie Frye?" Josh asked.

"Well, remember I told you that Spring-heeled Jack faded away. He probably died or was hunted down by vigilantes – or he only existed in the imaginations of these hysterical women. However, some of the old legends say he had a son. You'll never guess who that was," Selma smiled.

"Who? Batman?"

"No, he came much later. Who was the most legendary, infamous killer in old London?"

"Jack the Ripper?"

"Bingo! Jack the Ripper."

"Wasn't he real, though?" Josh asked as he furrowed his brow.

"Oh, he most certainly was, but there is this: he was never officially identified or even actually caught – was he? He just disappeared – like Spring-heeled Jack. The legend, undocumented, of course, is that the vigilantes hired a syndicate to eliminate Jack the Ripper. The Syndicate was a group of assassins, including Jacob Frye and his sister Evie Frye. The authorities considered these gangs "good assassins" because they only eliminated the "bad guys." According to legend, these citizen groups hired Jacob and Evie to kill Jack before he could murder any more innocent women."

"Like bounty hunters," Josh offered.

"Exactly right! Anyway, as the story goes, Jack was once part of the assassin syndicate himself but fell out of favor because he collected body parts for medical research. Jack was a doctor and was convinced that physical organs influenced insanity. Jack found out about the plan, so he decided to take action on his own. Some of the stories say that Jack was a surgeon at the London Insane Hospital called Bedlam. Jack captured Jacob while Evie was out of town and hid him in the basement of Bedlam Asylum. He knew Evie would come and rescue Jacob, so Jack waited. When she showed up, Jack planned to kill them both."

"What happened?" Josh asked.

"It didn't work out the way he planned," Selma said. "The twins killed Jack the Ripper, and that's why no one ever caught him. I think our killer has become so obsessed with Assassin's Revenge that he cannot separate reality from his game world. He identifies with Spring-heeled Jack, and he has a motive. They killed his son Jack the Ripper, so this Jack wants revenge. That's why he is after Evie Frye."

"Where does Batman figure into all these stories?" Josh wondered.

"He comes much later. Some say Jack the Ripper was Spring-heeled Jack's son and that Batman was his great-grandson. That explains why Batman does not kill – out of guilt for his violent family history."

"But, what do the manikins have to do with it?" Josh asked.

"They aren't manikins to Jack," Selma said.

"What are they, then?" Josh furrowed his brow.

"I don't know yet," Selma whispered, "but we've got to find out – and soon!"


Evie did not take long to find the cabbie who dropped Jack and Jacob off in front of Bedlam Asylum. Evie knew that Jack was holding her brother prisoner deep in the dank darkness of Bedlam Asylum. As if that would stop her from saving Jacob, Evie laughed.

Evie crept through the fog-shrouded night and across the wet grass behind the hospital. She paused against the brick wall to listen for sounds of movement from within. Small basement windows, half sunk into window wells, lined the outside wall of the hospital. They were not large enough to use as an entry or escape route. Nevertheless, she checked each one to see if the staff had fastened them securely – they had. Evie could hear the pitiful moans and often the screams of poor souls held within. She wished Jacob would make some noise, so she could at least locate him. Jack was too smart for that.

Evie was not naïve; she knew that Jack expected her to come to Jacob's rescue. She knew Jack intended to kill them both if he could. A trap usually only works if the victim does not expect an ambush. However, Evie was fully aware of Jack's intentions. She was prepared. The only one ensnared tonight would be Jack the Ripper.

If Evie could not get in below, she would get in from above. Few would expect an intruder to break into an asylum in the middle of the night by way of the front door. She quietly climbed the stone steps to the large entrance. A quick twist in the lock freed the latch. Evie entered the quiet hallway and quickly donned one of the white coats that lined the wall. She crept along the darkened corridor to the lighted nurse's station. She peered around the corner and saw that the night nurse was asleep in her chair. Evie ducked below the counter and slipped past the station to the hallway stairs.

The building was old, and the stone stairs did not emit a sound as she descended into the darkness. While the main floor was clean and well lit, the basement was the literal pit of hell. Dark, dirty, and stinking of excrement, the cellar was the dungeon of the hospital. It was where they kept the criminally insane – those poor souls no one cared for or even asked about them.

Evie slid silently down the hallway, pausing to let her eyes adjust to the darkness. She passed cell after barred cell of cages housing sleeping inmates. The cells were so full; some patients were sleeping on the cold stone floor. Moans and cries sounded throughout the basement. Civilized people did not keep animals so cruelly.

She took a metal coin from her pocket and tapped on an iron bar three times, then two in rapid succession. Jacob would know the code. Not hearing a response, Evie progressed farther down the darkened hallway. She paused at a corner that dead-ended at a stone wall. Evie tapped the nearby bars again. Not hearing a response, she worked her way back the way she had come.

Was Jacob lying cold and injured, unable to answer her taps? Was Jack waiting for her down here in the darkness? This could be the perfect trap. Jack would corner Evie and Jacob in a hallway with no escape – a dead end. Confident that Jack would not spring his surprise until she was boxed in again, Evie slowly moved toward the far wall ahead. Alone in the darkness, she worked her way from cell to cell, each dimmer than the one before. She steadied herself against the bars of an unseen cell as she tapped again. No response.

A hand emerged from the darkened cell behind her and clamped securely over her mouth. Unable to scream, Evie slammed tightly against the cell bars. She could not breathe. Who had her? Was it Jack holding her so brutally? Was it a crazed lunatic with evil on his mind?  Could it be Jacob?

"Quiet!" a raspy voice ordered. It was not Jacob! "Quiet, lass! I'll throttle you where you stand."

Gradually, the hand against her mouth eased enough to let her breathe. Evie realized Jack would have killed her already. She felt relieved – an inmate – she could handle that.

"Let me go," she mumbled against the filthy hand that covered her mouth.

"Not yet, young one. Not quite yet – I've plans for you – I do." He released Evie just enough for her to speak, yet his other hand reached through the bars. She felt cold fingers circle her neck.

"What plans, sir? I'm just a nurse come to see to your comfort," she pleaded.

"My comfort?" he croaked. "Since when? No one's cared a tinker's damn about my comfort since I been here," he laughed in derision. He lowered his voice to a hoarse whisper. "Quiet, now. Quiet now, or ye'll never speak again." He tightened the grip on her throat again.

"I'll be silent, sir," she choked. "I truly will," she lied. Evie felt the pressure on her throat ease, and the hand on her mouth lifted slightly.

"You must swear to help me," the inmate ordered.

"I shall," Evie promised. "What would you have me do?"

"It is true I am in an asylum, but I am as sane as you – maybe saner as I am not the one here of my own free will. You must get a message to the Queen straight away. I am with Her Majesty's secret police. She is in grave danger. They mean to kill her this very night," he warned, urgency in his hoarse whisper.

"If you will let me go," Evie promised, "I will do as you say."

The inmate spun Evie around to face the bars as he kept the tight grip on her throat. He brought his face as close to Evie's as he could and rasped, "You are not a nurse, who are you?" he demanded. "Do not lie to me," he warned ominously. "Are you an assassin?"

"I am Evie Frye," she told him.

The inmate's eyes became wide as the whites glowed eerily in the darkness. "You are one of them!" he barked. "One of the assassins!" his voice rose above a whisper.

The grasp on her neck grew tighter and tighter as the inmate became intent on throttling her. Evie strained hard to back away from the choking hand. She grew light-headed as she stared back at the lunatic in a desperate attempt to tell him that he was not Evie's intended target. Suddenly, the grip on her throat grew lighter and eventually eased off altogether. Maybe I will not die, after all, she thought. The inmate's eyes glazed over as a small trickle of blood appeared in the corner of his mouth. Gradually, the inmate's hand fell away from Evie's throat altogether and fell heavily back inside the bars. Motionless, the inmate slumped against the bars and slid down into a rapidly growing pool of blood at his feet, his eyes still staring at Evie as he died.

Jacob stepped from the darkness as he extracted his bloody knife from the hapless inmate. "Come on," he urged. "Let's get out of here. I know where Jack is." The cell was conveniently unlocked – also part of Jack's plan.

"This way leads to the back door," Jacob whispered. "He is lying in wait for us there. How did you get past him?" Jacob asked.

"I came in through the front door," Evie replied.

Jacob laughed. "That's the girl! Enter the way you are least expected. Jack does not know you came in through the front. He planned to drug you and throw you into the cell with our friend here, who would throttle us both. He was quite insane and a dangerous murderer. The cell was left unlocked so that our friend could escape after the deed. Later they planned to kill him too."

Evie followed Jacob up the darkened hallway to the main corridor. They paused at the steps leading to the main floor. "You must go back up and enter through the back door as he expects," Jacob instructed Evie. "Jack does not know the lunatic is dead or that I am out of the cell. When you enter, he will attack you, and I will strike as you grapple with him," Jacob whispered. "He will think that the inmate is still guarding me. He won't expect me to be there."

As Evie climbed the stairs to the main hallway, Jacob secreted himself in a dark alcove below. She snuck past the nurse on duty and hung the medical coat on the rack as she went outside. Evie found her way around the building and pretended to sneak into the back door. She intentionally fumbled with the handle so that Jack would know she was coming. She paused, inhaling a deep breath into her lungs, and slowly pushed the wooden basement door open.

Jack grabbed Evie before she could jump back and clamped the chloroform rag against her mouth. Evie held her breath until she felt herself falling into a swoon. Where was Jacob? She fought her attacker as blackness grew darker than the hallway surrounding her.

As the plane landed at Orlando International Airport, Selma made an announcement that shocked Josh. "I have a plan."

"What plan?"

"I'm going to Comic-Con dressed as Evie Frye."

# 20

As Selma and Josh trekked through the parking lot to the exhibit hall entry, Josh made up his mind about Selma's plan.

"Absolutely not!" Josh was adamant. "There is no way you are going to dress up as Evie Frye and bait this guy into abducting you!"

"Why not?" Selma argued. "We don't know who he is, but we sure know who he is after. Besides, you'd keep me in sight every minute. If something happened, you'd be able to step in and take the guy down."

Josh stopped beneath a palm tree in the middle of the Orlando Convention Center parking lot. "Selma, look," the situation was so unusual; he could not help but chuckle. His laugh came out more sarcastic than he intended. "We are so far out on a limb here – it's ridiculous. We are both out of our jurisdiction. In Florida, that's problem enough, but entrapment? That would kill our case even if we caught him – you know that! If we wanted to arrest a suspect, we'd have to call a local officer."

"Then, why are you laughing?" Selma demanded.

"Because it's so far out," Josh replied. "Man! We came here – you know, I'm not sure why we came here. No crime has been committed here for us to investigate! We don't even know who we're looking for. For all we know, he could be in that van right there," Josh pointed.

"He could be," Selma agreed, deciding to take the situation to the limit. "Let's check it out." She moved through a line of parked cars toward a white van.

"Selma, come on," Josh pleaded as she slowly approached the white van. "We've got no reason to suspect the owner of this truck."

"Look, Josh, it has a wheelchair lift! And the windows are all tinted, so you can't see inside."

"Right to privacy," Josh reminded her.

"I don't think anyone is inside," Selma reported after peering through the windows.

"Selma, stop, please. This is not the way to do this," Josh pleaded.

"Damn! Texas plates," she mumbled.

"See? Now leave that van alone, and let's go inside.

Selma scrunched up her face as she looked the van over. "Something's funny about this van, Josh."

"What? You said it was from Texas – not California. It's probably some guy at the convention. Maybe he brought a disabled child to meet comic book heroes."

Selma shook her head, "No. Something seems odd. Look at the plates – it's like they are brand new."

Josh put his arm around Selma's shoulder and brought her close. "You're grasping at straws. You're desperate. Desperate people make mistakes. We've already implicated one innocent person. Do you want to go for two?"

"This is my last chance, Josh. If we don't find him here, I have to go back to San Antonio. Thorn already told me, and I promised him that Orlando would be the end of it. I can't go back on my word," Selma said, her eyes growing damp with frustration.

"I know," Josh soothed her as he pulled her close, moving her away through the parking lot. "Look, let's stay on your plan," he reasoned. "It's a good plan and one that won't end up with an unhappy ending. Like you said, let's go inside and find a couple of Evie Fryes and follow them to see what happens. If one of them gets abducted, we can take some action. We'd have some probable cause then. We've got no reason to search that van. What if he's in there with a gun? He could shoot us through the windows right now."

Selma looked back at the van as she walked with Josh toward the auditorium entrance. "I know you're right," she reluctantly agreed.

"And while we're talking sanity, this plan to dress up like Evie Frye is crazy. I don't want you to do it – at least not here. It's too risky. Besides, we don't even know if he will show up here. I've checked the program, and Buck Russell is not on the ticket this time. He canceled. Maybe the killer's trigger is not Evie but Buck Russell. Couldn't that be?"

"Yeah," Selma had to agree. Every abduction so far had featured the popular movie character on the program. Maybe Josh was right. She knew he was right about their lack of authority. Perhaps she was getting a little too desperate.

Inside, they asked reception if they could see the director of the Orlando Comic-Con. An official escorted them to the office where Tobyn Sanchez was directing the show. "Good luck," their escort grumbled as he left them at the door.

They could hear Sanchez before they could see him. "Get fifty more chairs over to the show stage," he yelled as the two detectives walked into his office.

"Mr. Sanchez?" Selma asked.

Mr. Sanchez looked past Selma and Josh and ordered someone else to get a thousand more drink cups to the rear snack area. Then, he turned to a woman behind the desk and ordered her to check on a problem at booth 736; he was not kind about it. "Get your butt over there – now!" he barked!

"Mr. Sanchez, may we have a word?" Selma flashed her badge.

"Be quick about it; I'm buried up here," he gestured toward his neck. "What do you want?"

"We are checking up on an investigation, and we have some questions about how Comic-Cons are operated."

"What kind of questions?" The harried Mr. Sanchez interrupted Selma to scream at a nervous staffer standing nearby. "James! I told you an hour ago to get the back loading dock cleared." He pointed at a security monitor. "Does that look clear to you?"

"No, sir," James replied.

"Well, get out there and get all those people off my loading dock. Now!"

As James ran from the office, Mr. Sanchez turned back to Selma and Josh. "Well?" he shrugged, looking from one to the other, obviously expecting a question.

"We know you're busy; we're sorry to interrupt your work," Selma began.

"Look! Get on with it," Sanchez ordered. He opened his arms in front of him. "You see how it is. I'm sorry to be so abrupt, but what is it you need to know? Do we have a problem that involves the police here?"

"No. We just need some information. When people register for Comic-Con, do they tell you the characters they are going to portray?"

"Maria!" Sanchez shouted. "Come out here!"

A short, dark-haired woman emerged from behind a divider wall. "Yes, Tobyn, I heard. I'll handle it," she assured him gently.

She turned to the two detectives as Mr. Sanchez abruptly walked out of the office without a word. He left in the same direction James had gone.

Maria smiled. "Please excuse my husband," she pleaded. "He is very busy and very much under pressure, you understand. This is his first Comic-Con, and he is desperate for it to be a success. His career depends upon it, you see? He is not normally so snappy."

"I know," Selma nodded. "We came at a bad time – everyone is busy."

"This investigation you spoke of, does it involve our show?"

"No, ma'am. It's a case from another Comic-Con in another state," Selma assured her. "A young woman was abducted."

"Yes, we heard. Denver, yes? That man – that stuntman – he was the killer?"

Selma flinched at the mention of the stuntman. "No, Mrs. Sanchez. He wasn't the guy – someone had stolen his identity."

"Oh," Maria sighed, "and you want to make sure that does not happen here. No?"

"That's right," Selma assured her.

"Of course, I'll help all I can. Come back to my desk." She led the way to her work area behind the room divider and offered them a seat.

"Now, please ask your questions," she offered.

"When people come to Comic-Con, do they tell you what characters they are going to dress as?"

"Oh, goodness, no," Maria laughed. "We'd never be able to keep up with all that. We do have rules about dress and conduct. They come in any costume they wish. Sometimes they change the next day. You know some of these girls want to show too much – some of the men, too. Sometimes you can't tell the difference," she admitted with a giggle. "But no, they can come as they wish."

"So you wouldn't know, for instance, how many Batmen there were on a given day?"

"Many," Maria spread her arms. "No, I could not give you a number. It is not part of the registration."

"What about the vendors?"

"We know what the vendors are selling, but we don't know how they are dressed. There are rules for that, too," she assured them.

"Do you have a list of attendees?"

"Yes, we do have that – unless they bought their ticket with cash. It takes a few days for all the online tickets and credit cards to clear, but eventually, we will know the names of most of the vendors and participants."

"So," Selma reasoned, "you couldn't tell me if there was a character named Evie Frye here today?"

"I might be able to tell you if Evie Frye bought a ticket or a booth."

"No, I mean a character called Evie Frye," Selma explained.

Maria shook her head, "No, I am sorry. There would be no way to tell you that."


Selma and Josh walked up and down the aisles on the main floor, searching for Evie Frye. There was row after row of familiar characters, including some oddballs even Selma did not know. "Let's get a soda," Josh suggested as they approached the snack bar area. As Selma sat waiting for Josh to return with the drink, she spotted a girl, dressed as Evie Frye, sitting alone at one of the tables. She pointed her out to Josh as he sat two plastic cups on the table.

"See that girl," Selma pointed discreetly. "That is Evie Frye."

"Finally! I was beginning to think we weren't going to find one this time."

They watched as the girl sipped her drink. No one approached her, and she did not seem to be under any stress. She was just tired from winding her way among hundreds of booths. They decided to keep an eye on her just in case. Within fifteen minutes, two other Evie Frye characters passed by and moved off down the aisles.

"If you sit here long enough," Josh joked, "no telling who you'll see pass by. You want me to follow one of them," he pointed to the last one.

"Yeah, why not? I'll stay here and watch this one for a while longer," Selma said. "If something happens, call me, or I'll call you."

"Don't do anything without me," Josh warned Selma.

Josh moved off at a reasonable distance behind his Evie Frye. Evie Frye did not move or change positions for ten minutes until the girl's cell phone rang. Selma was not close enough to hear the conversation, but the girl became very agitated after a few minutes. Selma could read her lips saying "no" every few seconds. Ending the call, the girl angrily threw her phone into her purse, crammed her drink cup into the nearest trashcan, and moved off down the aisle toward the front of the convention.

Josh answered on the first ring, "Yeah."

"She's on the move – Row 15 – headed toward the front – I'm behind her," Selma reported.

The girl moved toward the front of the building without looking to the left or right. Passing the last booth, she entered the lobby and walked toward the main entrance doors. She went outside and stood on the curb. Selma stopped some twenty feet behind her and waited. The girl kept looking down the driveway, clearly expecting someone to drive through and pick her up.

Before Josh could show up, a white van made its way down the curving driveway beneath the palm trees. It stopped in front of the girl. The van had a wheelchair lift! Before Selma could react, the girl opened the door and hopped into the truck.

"Stop!" Selma yelled as the van pulled away from the curb. "Stop!" she yelled as she ran towards the vehicle.

Selma could hear Josh yelling her name behind her, but there was no time to wait. She raced into the driveway in front of the vehicle. The van rocked to a screeching halt as Selma flashed her badge and yelled, "Police!" Selma caught a glimpse of Texas plates as she moved around toward the driver's window.

The driver's window slowly came down, as Selma saw the shaken expression of a wide-eyed middle-aged woman staring out. "What's the matter, officer? I just came to pick up my daughter," she said in stunned amazement.

# 21

Jack could hear a man and woman arguing outside his van in the Orlando parking lot. They were three rows away, and Jack could almost make out their every word. A newly married couple arguing with each other at the place where they should be happy, he mused. What would the children think?

Jack tried to read his book as he lay in the rear of the van, but he thought he heard one of them mention "Evie Frye." Immediately on the alert, Jack laid the book aside and listened closer. They were arguing about something. She wanted to do something, and he did not want her to do it. On edge, Jack kept as quiet as possible. He caught the words "suspect" and "case" very clearly. Jack realized this was no couple arguing about which park to visit. These were cops. Jack reached into a compartment and charged a round into his .45 automatic.

Jack tensed when his van suddenly became the subject of interest. He watched through the perforated vinyl window coverings as the couple approached. This was bad. Jack realized he was going to have to kill a couple of cops.

They were right outside his doors arguing about probable cause. Who talks like that, except cops? Suddenly two hands pressed against the glass as a woman's face peered through the side window. Confident that she would not be able to see inside the darkened van, Jack held the cocked pistol centered right in the middle of her forehead. With his other hand, Jack silently snapped a picture of Selma's face with his cell phone. If worse came to worse, Jack would shoot her first and the man next. He would escape on the freeway before anyone knew what happened. As Selma moved back from the van, he followed her with the gun as she walked toward the rear bumper.

Jack heard the man say, "Selma, stop. This is not the way to do this."

Selma! Now Jack knew her name. He breathed a sigh of relief when Selma noted the Texas plates. Still, she was not satisfied. The license plates were too new, she thought. Jack listened as the man tried to reason with the policewoman. "Josh," she called him. The man's name was Josh. "You better listen to Josh, Selma – if you want to live," Jack thought as he trailed the handgun from one head to the other. He wanted Josh's picture too, but he was too far away from the van. Still, Jack memorized his face.

Jack figured out from their conversation that they were the same investigators who had connected him to Buck Russell. She said Orlando was her last shot to trap the killer. With that information, Jack knew they were not from Orlando – they were probably out of Denver. He learned that they would trail an Evie Frye character to try to trap Jack in the act. Jack was not going to let that happen. He had other ways of getting Evie Frye to leave voluntarily. The game was getting interesting, though, he thought.

"Yes, you are right, Mr. Josh," Jack thought as the couple moved away from his van. "I could kill you both right now, but this is much more intriguing," Jack smiled. "Besides, either way, it's going to turn out the same – Evie Frye in my van, and both of you dead."

Back inside the great hall, Josh and Selma decided to separate. "You're not going to be jumping out in front of any more vans, are you?" Josh asked.

"Not unless I have to," Selma quipped. "Go on," she hustled him off, "I'm okay. I'll call you if I need you. This would be so much easier if I were dressed as Evie Frye."

"That's not going to happen," Josh told her.

"Not today, anyway," she agreed as she moved off down an aisle.

The afternoon was pretty much a bust as they wandered through the myriad of booths and program areas. They encountered each other a couple of times, but a subtle thumbs-up indicated that things were okay. Selma saw a character dressed as Jack the Ripper. However, a quick casual conversation revealed that he knew nothing about anyone filming a movie. The only Evie Frye characters she saw were girls accompanied by a swarm of girlfriends or older adults. No one knew anything about a video.


Colleen rubbed at the small stain on her Evie Frye costume in the bathroom mirror. She had dripped some ice cream on her collar. Satisfied that no one would notice, she exited the bathroom to hear her name called on the PA system.

"Colleen Holloway, please report to the information desk."

She found her group of friends nearby and told them goodbye. "I've got to go! My Mom is here to pick me up. It's almost time to close anyway," she told them as she said goodbye.

"Are you Colleen Holloway?" the man in the lobby asked.

Colleen smiled and responded, "Yes, I know, my Mom is here to pick me up. Thank you," she flipped her hoodie back from her head and headed toward the main exit.

"Miss Holloway," the attendant called her back. "This man is here for you. Do you know him?"

Colleen turned as the man approached her from the side of the room. "Are you Colleen Holloway?" he asked, already knowing the answer.

Colleen noted that he was dressed as a medic with the name of an ambulance company embroidered on his jacket patch. "Yes, sir," she responded.

"Miss Holloway, I don't want to alarm you, but – "

Alarmed, Colleen feared the worst. "What's happened?"

"Miss, don't get upset – it's your mother. She has been in a car accident. She's not badly hurt, but she can't pick you up. I'm here to take you to her at the hospital. Will you come with me? I'll take you there now."

"It's okay," she told the attendant as she walked away. "He's here to help me."

Despite the driver's words that her mother was not badly hurt, Colleen was nonetheless in a state of shock. Why didn't her mother call? Was she so badly injured that she couldn't phone? The EMT led her to a white wheelchair van double-parked at the entrance with the flashers blinking. On a sign fastened to the outside of the truck, Colleen could read "Gotham City Ambulance." Without a second thought, Colleen opened the passenger door and climbed inside. She did not notice the Texas license plates.

Selma and Josh were on the way to the airport the next morning when they learned that the police had found the body of a young girl in a local park. Selma and Josh looked at each other in disbelief. Getting directions from their GPS, they drove to the park instead of the airport. The local police didn't look closely at their badges as he allowed them to enter the crime scene. Everyone was waiting for the coroner, so the body still lay on the ground beneath a thin cover.

"Can we see her," Selma asked?

Selma caught her breath as the sheet was pulled back to reveal a young girl dressed as Evie Frye. Josh took over the questioning as Selma struggled to keep from sobbing. "Were there any witnesses?" Josh asked.

"Not very many," the officer pointed to a nearby picnic table. "Those two over there are preparing their statement about what they saw this morning. They're pretty skittish -- they were out here jogging in the park before work, I guess."

"Can we talk to them?" Selma asked.

The officer looked around, "I don't see my Sergeant anywhere, but I don't see the harm. Let me see those badges again." Surprised, the officer noted, "San Antonio, Texas, and Denver, Colorado? Who are you guys?"

"We're here gathering evidence. We think this is part of a series of murders in both of our cities. We think they are linked," Josh explained.

"Look, the coroner is here," the office pointed to a dark car that had just arrived. "I've got to supervise this. Go ahead and talk to them, but be sure to give us a briefing on anything you find out. Okay?"

Josh agreed, and together they went to the picnic table where two people were filling out report forms.

"Sorry to bother you," Josh interrupted as he flashed his badge. "Can you tell me why you were in the park this morning?"

"We run in the morning while it's cool," the man said. "We were resting here at this table before getting ready to go to work."

"I see," Josh nodded. "Can you tell me what happened?"

"Yeah," the man said. "This van drove up – "

"It was an ambulance," the woman added.

"Yeah, kind of like an ambulance," the man agreed. "It had a sign."

"What did the sign say?" Josh asked.

"City Ambulance or something like that," the man said. "It had a name, but I don't recall."

"Yeah, it did," the woman agreed. "It was Gotham City Ambulance."

Selma mouthed "Gotham" at Josh, who continued questioning the pair.

"What happened," Josh prodded.

"Well, the ambulance pulls up, and the passenger door opens, and the girl falls out on the ground, and she doesn't move or nothin'. The ambulance roars off and leaves her there! We rushed over to help her, but she was unconscious. We were scared, so we called the police. That's all we know."

"What did the ambulance look like?" Josh asked.

"It was a white van with a wheelchair lift on the side."

"Did you notice the license plates?" Selma asked.

"No, I'm sorry."

"They weren't Florida plates," the woman interrupted. "I don't know what they were, but they weren't from Florida."

"What color were they," Josh prodded.

"It was white with black letters."

Disbelief and shock shook Evie to the core. She looked up from her phone, "It's him," she said. "I just searched local ambulances – there's no Gotham City Ambulance in Orlando. It's a clear reference to Batman. Why didn't I write that van's license number down yesterday? Selma moaned. "He got her out by pretending to be an ambulance driver."

"Selma, that van we saw yesterday was not marked Gotham City Ambulance," Josh reminded her.

"Josh, he uses those press-on signs. He posed as a medic this time to get her out of the building."

"He's changed his MO?" Josh asked. "I thought they didn't do that. Once they have a signature, I thought they didn't change."

"No," Selma corrected. "They do all the time, but this one did not change his MO, Josh. Cosplay," Selma said, slowly realizing the implication. "He just changed his costume. He still killed Evie Frye."

# 22

A reunion with Thorn was the last thing in the world Selma was looking forward to, but he was waiting when she returned to the office Monday morning. He had enough brains not to gloat.

"Mornin'," was all he said as she slumped into the chair behind her desk. Selma returned his greeting with a look and a nod. She sat quietly, going through the mail and documents on her desk.

"You wanna tell me what happened?" Thorn prompted.

"Not much to tell," Selma admitted. "We missed him again. Thorn, I was close enough to put hands on his car, but I didn't know it."

Selma brought Thorn up to date on everything she and Josh had discovered during her absence. She told of the evidence they had uncovered in Denver that led to the mess with Buck Russell, about the call from the cop in Arizona, and the embarrassing raid on Russell's home. Selma told him they eventually realized that someone was going around pretending to be the stuntman – even going so far as to fake his personalized license plate.

Everything Selma had been holding back suddenly sloshed over like water from a bucket. She talked about Orlando and her deep disappointment at letting the killer slip through her hands, about how she frightened a mother picking up her innocent daughter and how embarrassed she was about it. She told him how she found the strange van in the parking lot with Texas plates. She described her heartbreak at discovering a fresh victim in the park the next morning. She left nothing out. Selma hung all of her failures on the line for Thorn to see.

Thorn listened without interrupting. He knew the feeling.

When she finished talking and lapsed into silence, Thorn began to speak. "Back in my early days, I was young and still new on the force. Rangell was my partner, so you know how long ago that was," Thorn said with a sardonic laugh. We had a case – I was certain who did it – I had arrested him several times when I was on patrol – domestic violence mostly. He lived on my old beat. He beat up his wife on a regular basis. We tried to keep him locked up, but the judges kept turning him loose. We tried every way we knew to get that girl to leave him – go into a shelter. She wouldn't. She was a young girl from a good family, but even her parents couldn't get her to leave that rat bastard."

"One day, he took it too far, and he killed her in a fit of jealous rage. We knew who he was; all we had to do was pick him up, but we couldn't find him anywhere – we thought maybe he lit out for Mexico or something. So, we started leaning on his friends and what family he had around here. It got pretty rough – I wanted that guy so bad I couldn't sleep at night. It affected my relationship with my wife, and even Rangell got sideways with Bunny – that's how bad it was."

"The longer we hunted this guy, the more pressure we put on everyone around us. I hate to admit this, but we crossed some lines. We took his brother for a ride one night – unofficially. The brother wouldn't give him up, of course; he didn't give us a thing. He did file a complaint, and

174

Rangell and I got two weeks suspensions. We got too close
– too involved – too personal. It became a matter of pride.
You have to keep your distance, Cibolo. You can't get too
involved. It happens to us all."

"Did you get the guy," Selma asked.

"Yeah, but not the way we wanted," Thorn replied.
"They found him in a ditch one morning on the south side
with a .357 magnum round in his head. No one ever found
out who did it – probably a drug deal gone bad – or the
wife's family. I hope it was the wife's family."

" A .357 magnum? Isn't that what you guys carried
back in those days?" Selma asked.

Thorn ignored the implication. He stood and pulled
his sidearm out from under his jacket and laid it on the
desk. It was a .357 magnum revolver. "What do you mean
'those days'?" he laughed. "Still do," he grinned. "Best
damn law enforcement gun ever invented," he grinned.
"It'll stop an elephant," he claimed. "Point I'm tryin' to
make, Cibolo, is that we all get too close sometimes. It's
part of the job. It's gonna happen. It's unavoidable. Those
two weeks forced us to cool off enough that we didn't go
do something stupid – like killing the guy if that's what's
on your mind," he said pointedly.

"I didn't mean to imply …" Selma began.

Thorn waved her off. "I get it – no offense. I'm just
sayin' you've got to learn when it's time to cool off.
You've been on the force almost three years now. Have
you taken any vacation since?"

"I just came back from Disney World," Selma made
a weak joke.

"No, I mean, have you taken any time for yourself?"

"No. I was studying for the test. Then I got this job, so no, I haven't been off in a long time."

"You're not going to like this, but I want you to take two weeks off." Thorn spread both of his hands out in front of himself to try to hold her off. "Wait," Thorn pleaded, "think about it. I know the pressure you've been under and how it's affecting you. I'm not asking this for you – I'm asking for me."

"I knew you were going to try to take me off of this case," Selma snapped.

"Selma, it's not like that; calm down. I'm not taking you off the case," he assured her. "I'm just trying to give you some space to decompress. Rangell thinks you're close to cracking this case, and I agree with him, so just hold on a minute."

Selma eased back into her chair, still smarting from the thought that all her work may have been for nothing. She let the words sink in. "Rangell thinks I'm on to something?"

"Yeah, four murders add up to something – we don't know what, but we think you might."

"So, why the two weeks off?"

"Because of the way you are acting right now. Don't you see it? It's affecting you emotionally, and you don't even know it. We're afraid that if you get too balled up, you'll end up making mistakes. So we want you to take a couple of weeks away from the office."

"What about the case?" Selma asked. "What about those murdered girls – what about them?"

"San Antonio Comic-Con is coming up in a month," Thorn reasoned.

"Yeah, what about it?" Selma shook her head.

"When you come back, clear-headed," he stressed, "I'm assigning you to this case full time. The case is yours. We'll provide backup, but you can work it full time until the case is resolved or you reach a dead-end – **if** you take the two-week offer," he added quickly.

"What are the conditions and restrictions?" Selma asked suspiciously.

"Well," Thorn shrugged. "You need to rest," he stressed. "You can't come to the office or track down leads. You can go anywhere you want and do anything you want. Go to the coast, hang out on the beach, whatever. We want you to relax – do something you enjoy. You come back here rested and in a good state of mind, and the case will be here waiting for you."

"Is that a promise?"

Thorn nodded, "It's as close to a promise as I can get. I don't call the shots around here, but Rangell and I have discussed it, and that's the plan."

"Is this a suspension?"

"No!" Thorn insisted. "No suspension – it's a vacation. I know you aren't familiar with it, but a vacation is where people leave work – with full pay – I might add – and go away and do fun things. Go see your family, go visit relatives, go to the movies – anything you want," Thorn joked. "Go have some fun."

"Starting when?" Selma asked.

"Starting right now," Thorn said. "Go home. Take off that badge and gun, and do something to clear your head. Go do something you like to do – something you enjoy."

Selma sat thinking as new thoughts whirled around in her mind. "Maybe I'll just do that," she finally agreed. "Thanks, I appreciate it," she smiled.

Thorn sighed in relief and held out his hand toward Selma. She took his much larger hand in hers and shook it.

"No," Thorn nodded his head toward her belt. "The badge," he indicated her shield.

"You want my badge?" Selma recoiled. "I thought this wasn't a suspension," she accused.

"It's not, but I know you! Gimme your badge. I know I don't have a right to take it, but I'm just playing it safe here."

Selma pulled the badge holder from her belt and looked at it. "I thought you knew me better than that," she accused.

"I do," Thorn nodded. "That's why I want the badge. You don't give up – that's what makes you so good," he laughed good-naturedly. "I know you can buck me on this – go up to Rangell, and he'll probably let you keep it. But I'm asking, as a partner, please give me your badge," Thorn pleaded.

Reluctantly, Selma handed Thorn her badge. He said the one word she needed to hear. "As a partner," she repeated, still not fully convinced.

Thorn watched from the window as Selma got into her car.

"You know what she's going to do, don't you?" Rangell said from behind him as they both watched her put the car into gear.

"What?" Thorn snapped.

Rangell placed his hand on his friend's shoulder. "Same thing we would have done when we were her age," he mused.



Selma called Josh before she was out of the parking lot.

"Detective Logan," Josh answered the phone.

"Take a two-week vacation and meet me in San Francisco," Selma said.

"What?"

Selma repeated herself. "They want me to take two weeks off to decompress. They think I've been working too hard. They want me to go do something fun – something I enjoy," she added.

"What are we going to do?" Josh asked.

"I don't know about you," Selma laughed, "but I'm going to do something I haven't done in years."

"What's that?" Josh inquired.

"This weekend, I'm going to dress up like Evie Frye and go to the San Francisco Comic-Con!"

# 23

Jack planned his next move, back safe in his hideaway in remote west Texas, far from any big city. He reviewed the events of the past few days and realized that the cops were closing in. Jack recognized the need for more caution. Downloading Selma's picture from his phone, he transferred it to his computer and made a print. Her face was not that difficult to remember. Josh's face was etched in his memory. He would keep a close eye on these cops for sure. He assumed they would be in San Francisco. Confident that he knew them, but they did not know him, Jack thought that maybe he could take care of them there. End of the investigation, he laughed. It would be almost as fun as killing Evie and Jacob.

Using his new computer identity and after the briefest of research, Jack learned his cops were Selma Cibolo out of San Antonio and Josh Logan from the Denver police. Finding Josh's picture on the internet, he downloaded and printed a copy. Jack plotted to retire them both from the police force – from cops to corpses. Jack laughed at his little joke. Jack realized that both would be out of their jurisdiction in San Francisco – just as they had been in Orlando. They did not have the authority to arrest him unless they were part of a joint task force. That was unlikely. He wondered if he would see them at the next Comic-Con in San Francisco.

Jack checked his arrangements in San Francisco. The lease on his hideaway there was ending, so he would need to go to the Bay City a day early to renew. His Texas plates were still valid, so he made a mental note to return to Marfa on his way to San Antonio the week after the Frisco

Comic-Con. Jack toyed with the idea of driving up to Oregon to register the van there. That would throw them off, but he decided it would be unnecessary. If they had his plate number, someone would already be knocking on his door.

Instead, Jack decided to drive directly to San Francisco from Texas. On the way back, he would stop in Marfa to validate his plates. Jack was sure that the clerk was waiting on the corrected copies of his documents. He would not disappoint her. With comic-con in San Antonio, the Texas plates would blend right in with all the rest. If anything happened in Texas, he decided to set up operations in Los Cruces after the San Antonio event.

Satisfied that he had planned well, he intended to leave for San Francisco the next evening. It was three more days before the Bay Area Comic-Con. If he could trap the two cops there, his pursuers would be dead, and Jack would be free – free to get the revenge that kept him from perpetual rest.


The spirit of Spring-heeled Jack moved effortlessly through Bedlam Asylum. He floated free and unimpeded by bars, walls, or even darkness. Dark entities had summoned him from the grave with the knowledge that his son would get his revenge this night against the duo who had tormented him for so long.

Jack floated unseen through the darkened corridors and cells, searching for his son. In a matter of seconds, he had searched the entire hospital. In the basement near the rear entrance, he found Evie in the tight clutches of Jack the Ripper. Jack tried to warn his son of the unseen Jacob but could not make his voice leap the void between the spirit world and the living. Spring-heeled Jack's heart soared as he watched Evie struggle in Jack's arms. Any moment she would go limp, and her doom would be final. Her brother would be next.

The thought occurred to the ghostly Jack as he wound in and around the struggling pair, "where was Jacob?" He certainly was not in one of the cells. Instantly, Spring-heeled whirled again through all the asylum cells until he found the dead body of an inmate crumpled on the floor. He hovered to examine the body. Yes! This was the work of Jacob Frye. He killed his cellmate to escape. Where the devil was he now?

Racing back to the rear entrance, Jack arrived just in time to see the body of Evie Frye go limp and drop to the floor. Jack the Ripper grabbed the lifeless girl by the hair and dragged her down the dark hallway toward Jacob's cell. Jack struggled with Evie's dead weight, trying to get her through the cell door and over the dead body in the doorway. "Damn that lunatic," he said aloud. "He's already killed Jacob and left. I wanted Jacob alive so he could see me destroy his sister," he cried aloud.

"And so he is," came a voice from a darkened corner. Too late, Jack realized that the dead body on the floor was not Jacob Frye. Jack dropped Evie's limp body to the floor and assumed a defensive posture, realizing his immediate danger. He knew Jacob would pounce at any moment.

Swirling aloft, the ghost of Spring-heeled Jack watched, invisible and unheard – unable to help his son as the evil twins sprang their trap. Jacob pounced from the dark corner as Jack parried with his own knife. Each man held the knife hand of the other as the two men struggled in the gloom. The elder Jack looked on in horror as Evie slowly rose from the floor, knife in hand. She quickly plunged it between Jack's ribs and deep into his lungs. Jack released his grip on Jacob's hand. As quickly as a cobra, Jacob plunged his knife into Jack's heart. Jack the Ripper died as his body slid to the floor.

Above, Jack screamed his unheard agony into the darkness. Although she could not hear, Evie must have sensed his presence. Evie looked up in the direction of the whirling ghost, her face gloating with pride and victory. In his dream, Jack realized that she looked exactly like the picture of Selma Cibolo.

Selma was grateful that it was much cooler in San Francisco. Inside the heavy Evie Frye costume, she would have been broiling in Orlando. The cool ocean breeze was refreshing beneath the entrance awning while waiting for Josh to arrive. She had taken off her watch for the sake of the costume, but she could see from the tower clock in the park that it was after ten. Selma was annoyed that Josh was late. She toyed with the idea of peeking at her cell phone but decided against it. You never knew who was watching. All the while, she scanned the crowd for both Josh and Jack.

Too late, Selma realized the impetuousness of her plan. She felt obvious and exposed, waiting on the sidewalk. Even a casual passerby would know someone was coming. For Selma's idea to work, she must appear to be alone. Now, she had no choice but to stay in place; but they would develop a better plan next time. She moved behind a cement column so she could still see people coming and going, but they might not notice her. She made a mental note to get a room close to the convention center for the San Antonio event next week.

For now, the best she could hope for is that the killer would not spot her before she connected with Josh. She thought maybe she should go ahead, go in, and watch for him from there. She pulled out her cell phone and rang his number. It went to automatic voice mail.

"You lookin' for me?" said a voice behind her.

Selma spun and found herself face-to-face with Jacob Frye. "Josh," she cried, surprised, as she looked him up and down. "Jacob Frye! Are you kidding me?" she jibed.

In one of the most terrible cockney accents she had ever heard, he doffed his hat, bowed low, and said, "At your service, ma 'dam."

Certain that their cover was completely blown, Selma shook her head. Josh dropped the British accent and talked quickly. "I thought if I'm going to follow you around, it might be better if I looked the part. I remembered Evie had a brother, so I looked him up." He spun in a tight little circle, "What do you think?"

"I think it makes us look like we're together – not exactly what I planned," Selma admitted. "He only takes girls who are alone," she reminded him.

Crestfallen, Josh had to admit she was right. "Oh," was all Josh could say for a moment. Then, inspiration struck, "What if we came separately? I'll bet both characters show up at comic-cons all the time, and they don't even know each other. He wouldn't know we were together if we were separated," he reasoned.

Selma looked around with an amused smile on her face. "And, yet, here we stand on the sidewalk out front," she bantered.

"Right you are," he admitted. "Quick! Slap me!"

"What?" she said, shocked again.

"Slap me, like I tried to pick you up or something."

"As much as I'd like to, I'm not slapping you, Josh." It was such a bizarre idea it made her laugh. "Now go inside before someone sees us. Stay in sight but two or three rows apart. We'll see if we can salvage as much of this as possible," she laughed again despite her disappointment. "Why'd he have to be so cute?" she asked herself as he disappeared into the cavernous entryway. He did make a handsome Jacob Frye, she thought.

# 24

Selma pretended to shop through the vendor booths at the San Francisco Comic-Con Extravaganza. Josh managed to keep her in sight from two aisles away. Near the roasted nut stand, a body painter began decorating a cosplay body. He watched as a girl standing in a white cotton bikini beneath a cotton robe waited her turn as the painter finished painting his latest model. Both women were stunning. They were probably local models hired for the event.

One girl was nearly finished after having horns applied to her head. The horns looked like the horns of a kudu as they angled upwards into the air over her head. The airbrush artist had painted her skin to look like reptile skin. It was so realistic; Josh wanted to touch it to see if it was rough, but he knew he could not do that.

These women underwent an amazing transformation. Another woman emerged from behind the curtain. She was a cat. Her face was eerily human, and her body seemed covered with fine cat hairs. Josh knew it was an artistic illusion, but it seemed so authentic to the eye. Another artist posed the girl in the bikini and began painting flesh tone paint to her torso over the bikini. The color blended with her skin so closely that it looked like she were nude even from a close distance. These artists could do such amazing work, he thought before realizing that Selma had moved out of sight.

Selma browsed from vendor to vendor, pausing long enough for Josh to keep up with her. He was doing a great job – she could not even see him herself. She stopped at a comic cover artist display. He had drawn and painted hundreds of pictures of superheroes and imaginary beasts. She looked up and down the aisle but did not see Josh. She hoped he was keeping her under surveillance.

Engrossed in the cover art, Selma did not notice the character dressed as a Dark Avenger character Wolverine until he spoke to her. "Who are you?" he asked good-naturedly.

Selma looked him over quickly, not fully understanding his question. It was the way he asked that caused her some concern. He emphasized the "are." Was there more than one question there? He did not strike her as a killer, but still, Jack had changed costumes before – so Selma was on her guard. She tried to act nonchalant. "Evie Frye," she pouted. "Can't you tell?"

"Oh, I guess I don't follow that story," Wolverine admitted. "I don't come to these things very often," he added. "Who's Evie Frye?"

Selma smiled and shook her head, "It's a long story – it's from a game. It's stupid," she said, "but I liked the costume, so I thought I'd try it out. I don't really know who she is or what she does," Selma said, hoping he would get bored and go away. No such luck.

"Well, it's a very interesting costume; you do look very pretty in it. Are you here alone or with someone?"

Not wanting to reveal too much, Selma replied, "I'm here by myself, but I'm not alone. I'm meeting some friends later today."

The Wolverine looked at his feet and shuffled a little. When he looked up, he noticed that Selma was not paying attention to him. "Maybe …" he began, "maybe, we can go get a drink or something," he offered.

Selma shook her head, "Look, you seem very nice; but I'm really just here to look around and meet my friends. Thanks for the offer, but I do need to keep moving. It was nice meeting you," she said as she walked away.

Selma moved to the next booth, keeping her eye on the stranger. He shrugged and moved across the aisle to another vendor booth and began rummaging through the comic books stacked on the table. Selma looked for Josh but still could not find him. She went down the row and turned right to go down a different block of booths. Ten minutes later, Wolverine continued to watch her from down the walkway. Maybe there was more to this person than she thought. She changed aisles again, and so did Wolverine. He was following her. But, why?

Selma moved through the crowded event hall, eyeing all of the characters and creatures that came and went. There were about a dozen Harley Quinns in different costumes along with an assortment of Wonder Women. Ironman went by, accompanied by s dog, which was also dressed as Ironman. The Mad Hatter and Alice strolled by, but they were not having fun. Apparently, Alice thought the Hatter had noticed a few too many Poison Ivies. There was even a Quasimodo – what the heck was he doing here? Is Quasimodo in a game now? There were gremlins, goblins, and ghosts galore. A very impressive Dumbledore paraded around the signing booths. She passed Ace Ventura, that guy from Breaking Bad, and a Rachel from some movie.

The girl dressed as Hawkgirl was particularly fabulous. She had feathered wings that fell from her shoulders to her ankles. When she had gathered a crowd of eager photographers, she would activate a hidden button. Then, her wings would slowly rise until soft feathers completely encircled her body. It was something to see. Even Quasimodo was impressed.

Selma finally spotted Josh a few booths away. Making sure that Wolverine could not see her, Selma gestured to Josh, pointing out the Wolverine character making his way toward them. Then she pointed to the entrance, indicating that she was going to lure Wolverine toward the front. Selma slowly made her way toward the front, but apparently, Wolverine had lost interest and no longer followed her. She doubled back and found Josh now tailing Wolverine. Separated by the rows, Selma kept them in sight as she pretended to shop the vendor booths. Wolverine did not approach anyone else, nor did he seem to have any further interest in Selma at all. After half an hour, she decided that Wolverine was not a threat, and she signaled Josh to meet her at the snack bar.

"Who was that?" asked Josh as he sat at her table.

Taking a sip of soda, she replied, "Wolverine. Didn't you recognize him?"

"Who the heck is Wolverine?" he wanted to know.

"Man, you really do need me in this case, don't you?" Selma laughed. "Wolverine is one of the X-Men – a group of mutant misfits put together by Professor X – you know, like Gambit, Cyclops, Storm – characters like that. They fight for truth and justice!" Selma pronounced dramatically, striking a typical cosplay pose.

Josh put his hands to his face, "It's hard to keep up," he announced. "Is he a threat?"

"No, I don't think so," Selma admitted. "He just tried to pick me up – that's all. It seems like some guys don't have a clue," Selma quipped, but it went right over Josh's head. He seems like a nice guy – just looking for a little company. Our Jack has changed his costume before, but he's not going to get too far away from Jack and the storyline. These X-Men characters don't fit the scene. I'm sure Jack will stay with the Spring-heeled Jack theme."

Jack found an Evie Frye character moving among the vendor tables. This one was a little older than usual, but that did not matter. On a second look, Jack was amazed to realize that this Evie Frye was that cop from Orlando. This was too rich! She was playing right into his hands. Where was her partner? He must be somewhere near. Jack scanned the crowd looking for anyone that was out of place with the costumed characters. "Where was he?" Jack wondered, knowing that Josh Logan had to be around somewhere. They worked together, probably as part of a task force, Jack realized. A Jacob Frye character caught his eye. Jack looked closer. Yes! It was he. Now the pair were dressed as Evie and Jacob, trying to lure him into a trap – imagine that! That trap was not going to work. A snare only works, he thought, if the victim does not know it is a trap. They were going to have to get smarter than that.

Far from being intimidated, Jack was hatching a plan in his mind. This was working out very well, he thought – just like in the dreams. It was going to be so easy to lure them into a trap. Where? Not here. Slowly, Jack began to develop his plan around the setup in San Antonio. If they were chasing him in San Francisco and Orlando, they surely would be trying to capture him in other places. San Antonio? Yes! That would be much better. It would be the perfect setup. He already had all the elements in place – a remote location without many nosy neighbors around. It would be easy to lure the elusive Evie Frye to his lair on the outskirts of San Antonio. Once he had her, Jacob would follow. Jack knew just how to do it.

Jack was surprised to see her conversing with a character dressed as the Wolverine. Was he another assassin police officer? Jack knew that the Wolverine character was not part of the Syndicate storyline. Still, he was temporarily confused as to why Wolverine was even there with Evie. Jack watched as Evie turned away and worked her way down the row of vendors, pretending not to know him. Wolverine was a problem Jack would have to deal with before leaving San Francisco. Evie and Jacob could wait for San Antonio.

Following at a discreet distance, Jack watched as the Wolverine followed Evie. Boy! Is this bloke in for a big surprise? This is going to be fun. Soon he saw Evie signal to Jacob. Together they kept Wolverine in their sights. When Wolverine failed to follow Evie to the exit, Jack realized that Jacob had gone back undercover.

As Evie and Jacob continued to circulate the showroom, Jack realized they looked closely at all the Jack the Ripper characters. Jack immediately exited the front. Making sure no one was following, he secluded himself in his van. Quickly changing costumes, Jack emerged as an ambulance driver. He stretched on bloody sleeves to make it seem it was cosplay and returned to the exhibit hall.

Locating Evie and Jacob in the snack bar area, Jack sat nearby and improved upon his plan. Jack remembered that San Antonio was in her jurisdiction! Jack immediately realized that both officers were again out of their authority here in San Francisco. They could not arrest him here unless they had special powers from the local authorities. Jack's mind raced as he realized that although she would have jurisdiction in San Antonio, it would still be easier to get his revenge on them there. Jack was thrilled that he knew just how to do it. The dreams gave him the plan. It was perfect.

In his mind, the identities of Selma and Josh faded in Jack's mind as the two detectives became Evie and Jacob. He felt that events were falling into place. He would finally get his revenge. The others were not real; they were only imitations of Evie Frye. Those other girls meant Jack no harm. They did not even know who Spring-heeled Jack was. That was why eliminating them had brought Jack so little satisfaction. Now it was apparent. Here were the real Evie and Jacob Frye. They were out to destroy him, just as they had killed his son Jack the Ripper. These two knew who Spring-heeled Jack was. It was all too perfect. Now, he could carry out Jack the Ripper's plan to eliminate both Evie and Jacob together. Jack laughed at his brilliance. He was the master. Slowly, he faded back into the anonymity of the crowd and worked his way back to his van. After taking care of Wolverine tonight, he would drive to Texas, where he could finally fulfill all his dreams at last.

Selma returned to San Antonio three days before San Antonio Comic-Con. She did not tell Thorn that she had been to San Francisco. Of course, he asked had done during her time off; but Selma dodged the questions as much as possible. She went out of her way not to tell a lie. She mentioned lying on the beach and eating seafood, which was true – just not on the Gulf coast. Nor did Selma tell Thorn about her plan to dress as Evie Frye at the San Antonio event. She even avoided telling Thorn that Josh would be coming to Texas to join her. Selma did not want to get into the entrapment and evidence discussion. The less Thorn knew, the better. She intended to stop Jack from killing another girl whether she could get a conviction or not. For the remainder of the week, Selma performed her routine duties as if nothing was wrong. Her imagination drew her along twists and turns through Victorian London, but she was laying plans to trap a modern-day monster in the Alamo city.

# 25

Selma thought her idea to reserve a room near the event was a stroke of genius as she added the final additions to her Evie Frye costume. She looked into the mirror at Josh across the room. He was struggling to apply eye makeup. He was making a mess of it.

"Here, let me help you with that, cowboy! Don't you know how to wear mascara?"

"No, I don't," he grumbled. "I never wore mascara before. I don't see how you stand it!"

"What?" Selma pretended to be shocked. "You think I wear mascara? I'll have you know my eyes need no enhancement, sir!"

She enjoyed his flustered expression. Taking him off the hook, she asked a more serious question. "How in the world does your department let you go on these investigations out of town?"

He looked up at her as she applied the makeup, the brush an unnerving whir before his eyes. Any minute, she was going to put his eye out! He could not help but blink.

"Selma," he said earnestly, "you don't realize how important you are to this case. My department believes you are right on the verge of catching this guy."

"They may be the only ones; I wish my guys were as supportive. I might be getting through to Thorn, but even he has begun to press for a quick resolution. If we don't catch him soon, it may be all over for me. They could take me out of the game any day now."

"We'll get him," Josh said as he stood and looked at himself in the mirror. "Good job – I guess. Am I supposed to look like this?"

"Perfect," she assured him. "Now go on down, and I'll follow you in a few minutes. I'm glad we got rooms here in the convention hotel. We can arrive separately and not worry about anyone seeing us coming in together. Be careful down there. If you spot him, give a signal. I'll do the same."

Josh pulled his sidearm from beneath his cloak and checked that it was ready. Placing it back in his holster, he asked, "Have you got yours?" His police badge was affixed to the holster in case anyone questioned his carry.

"Of course," she said. "I just don't have to flash it around for effect," she teased.

Josh put his gun away and rubbed his stomach. "I've got a little indigestion – must have been that food from last night." He pointed to the bathroom door. "Do you mind?" he asked?

"Go ahead," she said. She could not help but tease him a little more when he emerged from the restroom. "Are you okay?" she laughed. "I told you to lay off those jalapeños."

"Yeah, I'll be all right. Just stay close to the restrooms, will you? Maybe after lunch, I'll feel better."

"Yeah, we'll have enchiladas – the hair of the dog," she teased.

"Not me! Never again," he vowed as he rubbed his stomach. "I'm sticking to barbeque."

She laughed as Josh left the room. He made a good Jacob, she thought. She allowed enough time for him to get down the elevator before she followed. Another good thing about this setup is they would not even have to go outside. It looked like rain. The hotel elevator slowly descended to the Comic-Con lobby at the civic center. The image in the elevator mirror reflected a convincing Evie Frye. The costume was perfect and fit her like a glove. Josh had probably reached the event floor by now and was probably ready to trail her discreetly as she searched the crowded rows for Spring-heeled Jack.

Just outside the main entrance, her cell phone rang out. She had forgotten to mute the ring tone. It caught her by surprise, and she struggled to get it out of her tight costume. It was Thorn. She stepped into a small alcove off the main lobby and answered.

"Hey!" he chuckled, "May I speak to Edie Frye?"

"It's Evie," Selma reminded him, annoyed. He can't even keep the name straight. "How did you know I was in costume?"

Thorn laughed. "I know you," he laughed. "And I know me – it's the kind of thing I would have done back in the day."

Selma laughed at the thought, "You'd have made an ugly Evie Frye." She laughed aloud.

"How little you know," he shot back. "I've been undercover in drag many times," he bragged.

"So that's where you go on Saturday nights," she teased. "I'm in the hotel," Selma told him. "I was just going down to begin circulating."

"You got your buddy with you?" Thorn asked.

Noting the insulation in his voice, Selma corrected him. "You mean Detective Logan? Yes, he checked in last night." Hearing Thorn chuckle, she added, "He has a room next door. You know, Denver gives him a much longer leash than you give me. They think I'm on to something here. I wish I had that luxury."

"Oh, you do," he assured her. "You got me. I believe you. If I didn't, you wouldn't be there. But still," he paused, "We've got to wrap this up before the brass shuts us down. You know that."

"I know," Selma admitted. "What about you, Thorn? Do you think I'm on the right track? Be honest – it's okay. I know I've pushed you to the limit."

"You have done that," he agreed. "But I do believe you. I've learned a lot about this cosplay stuff from you, and yes, it does make a great cover for a serial killer – I just never put it together that way. I'm not the only one who believes you either," he admitted.

"I know," she smiled. "Denver PD has been just absolutely amazing. Those guys have put up with a lot."

"Not only them," Thorn teased.

"Who else?"

"How about the Feds?"

"Well, they did raid Buck Russell's compound solely on our lead, but I guess they've changed their mind about that for now. I'm sure that was embarrassing for them and the agency."

"Don't think so," Thorn hinted. "I wouldn't be so sure."

"What do you mean?"

"Got a call from them this morning. In fact, they're thinking about taking over the lead."

Selma sighed. "It's just as well," she admitted. "I've probably used up about all my chips on this one. It's a wonder you've let me go this far."

"I wouldn't be so sure," Thorn told her. "Sounds like they still want you on the team if they do take over. Anyway, try to wrap it up this weekend if you can. I cannot spare anyone to back you up right now, but you have your Colorado *buddy* there. Even if he doesn't have jurisdiction – you do. If you need help, call for backup. I might come out myself if I have time."

"Thanks, I gotta let you go," Selma retorted, "my **buddy** is waiting." Thorn knew how to push her buttons.

Hanging up, Selma secreted her cell phone inside her costume. It was a tight fit. Despite the slight bulge, she did not think anyone would notice under the cape. She would try not to use it on the showroom floor. She would not make a convincing Evie Frye with a cell phone in her hand. Fortunately, the heavy topcoat concealed her gun bulge. Nevertheless, she showed her Comic-Con pass and her police badge to the ticket checker at the door and entered the booth area.

She did not see Josh anywhere around, but she did see Quasimodo again. Whatever game he was in must be getting popular – popular enough for a Quasimodo character to be in San Francisco and San Antonio only a few weeks apart. The various character's popularity rose and fell according to the popularity of their game.

"Where the heck is Josh?" she wondered. "If he's supposed to be trailing me, he's doing a fine job."

The usual cast of characters paraded around in a disorganized mob, and cosplay models cruised the hall, stopping only long enough for fans to take their picture. Selma wound through the usual cast of characters circling the booths and standing in line for autographs. She asked a few attendees, but no one had heard of any video filming taking place. No one had seen Jacob Frye either – which concerned Selma a little.

She doubled back, thinking that if he were following her, she might run right into him. She had no such luck. Josh was doing a great job of staying out of sight. Selma decided that she would mingle for a few more minutes, and if she did not spot him, she would check the restroom area. A few minutes turned into thirty before she finally caught sight of him coming out of the men's room.

"There you are! Where have you been?" she asked.

He pointed to the men's room door. "In there," he groaned. "Man, I've got it bad – it's this Tex-Mex food you are so addicted to."

"Montezuma's revenge," she laughed. "It'll wear off. You'll be chowing down on a chimichanga by lunchtime – you'll see.

"Not me! I'm staying away from that stuff. Give me an antacid and a stomach pump!"

They spent the better part of the morning circling the great hall but did not spot a single Spring-heeled Jack. She spotted two or three Evie Frye characters, but they had several friends with them – they were not the type Jack targeted. Jack wanted his prey to be cut from the herd. All of the Evie's she talked to told Selma that no one weird had approached them, and none of them had heard any rumor of a movie or film. Selma was disappointed. Was her last chance evaporating before her eyes? Where was the killer? Why didn't he try to make his move? Where was he? Selma believed that Jack would try to attack her and somehow get her out of the building. She wanted to make it easy for him by hanging around the darkened back door area, but no luck. She realized that Josh was not where he was supposed to be again – time to check the restrooms once more.

# 26

Spring-heeled Jack was thrilled to see Evie Frye and Jacob together in the crowd. The fact that they did not stay together played right into his hands. Nothing was going to stop Jack now. He had them both right where he wanted them. The dream was coming true at last.

Obviously, they did not know Jack was following them. It was hilarious; they thought they were stalking him. Jack noted that Jacob visited the men's room three times in the first two hours. Perfect! His plan was working out better than he had hoped. Getting to Evie was going to be so easy. Leaving the vast hall, Jack left the floor and exited the building. There were preparations to make.

Back in his van, Jack flipped off the hot mask and turned on the air conditioner. He sipped on a cool soda from his portable refrigerator and sat back to mull over his plan. Jack realized capturing them together would be impossible. But like in the dream, he would have to take one and lure the other into the trap, and he knew which one to capture first – just like in the dream.

He took out a blank sheet of paper and an ink pen as he considered how to construct a note. It would have to be cryptic but easy enough to solve. It would not do to host a party and have no one come. No, Jack thought, this party must have two guests of honor.

Pen in hand, Jack began to construct a note to lead the pair into a lethal trap. Jack decided it would be more expedient if he captured Jacob first and then tempted his sister to go to the rescue. It was perfect. If Jacob continued to be indisposed, so to speak, it would be so easy. He would spring his trap while Jacob Frye was least expecting. On his third draft, Jack had hit upon the perfect riddle. Using red ink, just like the famous Jack the Ripper note, he created a message with clues that no one could ignore.

Jack folded the note and decided that his medical outfit and the wheelchair would be his best bet. A wheelchair would be the best way to get an unconscious detective out of the big exhibit hall. Dressed as a medical person, Jack would not arouse unwanted attention. The trick was to get both Evie and Jacob separated with enough time to accomplish the snatch and make his exit.

Attaching the Gotham City Ambulance sign to his windows, Jack drove behind the exhibit hall to the loading dock. Jack had been there before – a couple of times. Pulling up to the gate, a security guard stopped him and came around to the side.

"Do you have an emergency?" the guard asked.

"No, sir," Jack responded. "I'm here to pick up a resident of the Gotham Nursing Home."

"Where the heck is that?"

"About sixty miles from here – down by Three Rivers," Jack lied.

"How long are you going to be back here?"

"Just long enough to pick up my rider; then, I'll be gone – twenty minutes tops."

"Okay. Park over there by the ramp," the guard pointed.

Back on the exhibit floor, Jack stashed his wheelchair in a small area next to the restrooms. Jack tried to keep an eye on both Evie and Jacob. It was not an easy task. It became obvious that they could not even keep up with each other. Jack watched Jacob enter the men's room, so Jack turned his attention to Evie. Jack followed her into the lobby and watched as she pushed the elevator button. She was going back to her room. Now was the time!

Selma pushed the elevator button and waited for the doors to open. She got off one floor early to make sure no one was following. When the door opened twice, Selma decided she was alone and pushed her floor number into the elevator keypad. Josh did not answer the knock at his door, and he was not in her restroom. Maybe Josh went back to his room to lie down.

She dialed his number and waited. She was prepared to say, "Where the heck are you," when Josh's phone on the other side of the room began buzzing. Oh! No! Josh did not have his phone with him. "Not good," she said to herself. Selma decided to go back down to the floor, carrying Josh's phone to give it to him herself – if she could find him.

Jack carefully and silently entered the men's room. He checked beneath the stalls and saw only one pair of feet. Jack waited until two men at the urinal finished their business, washed up, and left the room. Jack picked up the yellow closed for maintenance sign and placed it outside the door. "Sorry, guys," he told two men moving toward the door. "We'll have it open in a few minutes. We have a medical situation in there. It's pretty messy – you probably don't want to see that. We'll have it cleaned up in a minute. You might want to try another restroom if you can't wait." He pushed the wheelchair into the restroom and made sure he had blocked the door from opening, and concealed himself in the stall next to Jacob's.

As Jacob emerged from his stall, Jack quickly clasped his handkerchief over Jacob's mouth and nose. After a short struggle, Jacob slumped to the floor. Jack promptly pulled his limp body up and into the waiting wheelchair. Jack retrieved Jacob's top hat from the floor and folded the note inside. He left the hat neatly propped on the sink counter, pushed the unconscious Jacob out through the door and down the loading dock ramp.

As the wheelchair lift raised Jacob into the van, Jack was pleased to note that no one was following. All he had to do now was take Jacob to his lair and wait for his sister to come to rescue him. It was so easy it was funny, thought Jack as he drove away, laughing at the top of his voice.


Josh came awake slowly. His head hurt, and he was having trouble moving his body. Though groggy, it was apparent that he was no longer at the Comic-Con. He did not know where he was, but it was probably better to pretend that he was still under the spell of whatever drug that had knocked him out. Josh gradually opened one eye and peeked out at the scene. It looked like a barn, but no one was in sight. Some of the wallboards leaked light, and it fell into the room through the slats, creating crazy slanted shadows. He eased open his other eye so that it would adjust to the low light levels in the room. Yes, it was some sort of barn with a packed dirt floor. Large sharp hooks hung from the ceiling. The place smelled like dirt. Something chafed his wrists, and he could not move his arms or legs very far. He felt like he was lying on his stomach. After checking around the room for his captor, he tried to find out what was holding him. Josh did not see anyone in the room with him, so he grew bolder and more aggressive in moving his arms and legs. It was no good.

Josh's body swung weirdly as he realized someone had hoisted him up in the air in a sort of swing or harness. He was suspended spread-eagled from the rafters of the old barn, unable to move much of anything. He was in a type of sling, dangling from some of those hooks. His arms and legs were shackled to spreader bars that held his arms and legs outspread. As his eyes grew accustomed to the darkness, he began to make out more room features. A dim light coming from a hole in the roof helped some. If this was a ramshackle barn, but it appeared no one had used it in several years. Several small cages were stacked along the walls and haphazardly across the room. A long, narrow wooden table was in the center of the room. Near the table was a large stump with a rusty ax embedded in the top. It seemed to be a chopping block. It seemed to Josh like a butcher's table. What was it used for? Maybe something in the cages – chickens, perhaps, or rabbits.

Slightly beneath him, Josh saw a rough wooden table. Neatly lined up on the table, Josh noticed his badge, his handcuffs, and his handgun. The gun was near the edge of the table. If he could just reach the weapon, Josh would at least have a way to defend himself. Slowly and painfully, Josh stretched his right arm as far as it would go. No such luck – the .45 lay just inches away from his outstretched fingers. If he could get just a couple of inches closer, he could grab it.

Slowly, like in a backyard swing, Josh began to rock his body forward to build momentum. His body slowly swung closer to the table until the gun was tantalizing close at the end of each arc. Exhausted, Josh realized it was no good. He did not have enough slack to reach the weapon.

"You fool!" Jack taunted from the shadows. "You actually think I would leave a gun within your reach, Jacob?" Jack doubled over with laughter. "What would happen if you killed me?" he taunted as Josh's body swung wildly back and forth from the effort. "You'd hang there and starve to death. What then, Jacob? What would you do then? What would your sister say?"

"What sister? What are you talking about? My name is Josh Logan, I'm a police officer, and I'm placing you under arrest!"

Jack laughed even more at that. It seemed he would not stop laughing. Jack laughed so hard he had to sit in a wooden chair nearby.

"Yes! That's rich – I'm under arrest, am I? Really? You've been playing too many video games." After another bout of hysterical laughter, Jack grew serious. "You poor deluded sap! You are not a police officer! You are an assassin. You are Jacob Frye, and you have failed in your mission to murder me. Now the shoe is on the other foot, and you are my prisoner. We shall wait here for your sister, the infamous Evie Frye. She will be along directly to save your worthless hide, and then you will both be out of your misery. And, out of my way!"

"I told you my name is Josh Logan! I am a police officer with the Denver PD!"

"Denver?" Jack laughed. "Aren't you a little out of your jurisdiction? Besides, this is not police television. And, you are not exactly in a position to bargain. When your sister Evie arrives, you can watch as I take my revenge out on her."

"Revenge?" Josh asked. "Revenge for what? My partner's name is Selma! She's a police officer too – from San Antonio. She does have jurisdiction, and she's not my sister. We are in a costume – it was Comic-Con. That's what people do, go dressed as comic book characters."

"I know very well what you did!" Jack snapped. "Both of you ambushed and killed my son. Now, I have you trussed up like a calf about to be butchered; and soon, I'll have your sister too. You can watch," Jack promised. "By the end, you'll wish you were dead. Soon after – you will be!" Jack broke into another bout of hysterical laughter.

In the dark cavernous barn, the laughter seemed even more hysterical. It seemed to Josh to be the maniacal rantings of an insane man. Josh did not doubt that Selma would somehow figure out where he was and follow. That was what this madman had planned – he would make it easy for her. Josh knew he was the bait. She would walk right into his trap. Josh would do what he could to warn her before it was too late.

Josh inventoried in his mind what he had left in his pockets, not that it would do him any good. There was nothing within reach that he could use something to signal her about the danger. Maybe he could rattle the chains, but the sound was weak and did not carry. There was nothing. Even so, he would not have been able to reach far enough to use anything.

"I'll leave you now," Jack taunted. "Don't go off with anyone, you hear?" he laughed that insane laugh. "Just hang around and wait for your sister. I'll see you later."

Left alone, Josh continued to try to escape. He quickly determined that it was useless. Darkness began to overtake the room, making it impossible to see even the far wall now. The dim light coming through the roof was growing darker and darker. Flashes of lightning partially lit the building and just as quickly dashed it into darkness again. Josh wondered where his tormentor had gone. Was he hiding in the shadows – waiting? How was Selma ever going to find him? In the twilight, objects in the barn began to recede into the darkness until it became difficult to see even the long table closest to him.

Suddenly, he heard a loud snap as a dim light flickered on in the back of the room. Josh realized that Jack had installed one of those automatic battery-powered lights that came on in the dark. It was not much light, but Josh could see well enough to make out the door frame. As soon as Selma appeared, he was determined to warn her by shouting. As if Jack could read his mind, rough hands from the darkness behind jerked on his chain, and someone stuffed a rag into his mouth.

The gag smelled of gasoline and motor oil.

# 27

How long is he going to be in that bathroom? Selma nervously paced back and forth. She had not seen Josh in over an hour. If he is that sick, maybe he should go up to the room and lie down. The entire operation was in jeopardy. Selma saw her chances going up in smoke. In desperation, she stopped a young cosplayer dressed as the Joker before he entered the restroom door.

"Excuse me, young man. Can you help me a moment?"

"Sure, lady," he smiled. "What do you need?"

For some reason that stung, Selma realized that the boy considered her an older woman asking for help, but she brushed it off. "My friend is not feeling well. He went in there," she pointed, "and he hasn't come out in a long time. Would you mind checking on him for me?"

"Sure thing, ma'am. I'll be right back."

"His name is Josh," she offered as he disappeared behind the door. The kid did not come back for a few minutes. Selma guessed he had business to take care of himself. When he reappeared, he was carrying Josh's costume top hat. "No one's in there with that name, but I did find this hat on the counter. Is it his?"

Selma grabbed the hat, "Yes! That's part of his costume. Are you sure he's not in there?"

"There are two or three guys in there, but nobody named Josh."

Selma thanked the boy and sat at a table in the nearby snack bar area. Where is he? she wondered. Why wouldn't he have come to tell her if he was that sick? She placed the hat on the table and stared at it. Why would he leave his hat behind? It just didn't add up.

Puzzled, she absentmindedly tapped on the crown of the hat as she tried to decide what to do next. A small folded paper peeked from beneath the lining. Selma pulled it out and discovered a folded note.

Unfolding the note, Selma saw that the letters were in bright red ink. "Dear Boss," it began. Selma immediately drew comparisons with the famous Jack the Ripper letter. The writer had clearly modeled it on that historical note.

Dear Boss,                              Clue #1,048

I keep on hearing the police have caught me out in California, but they haven't fixed me just yet. It was quite a spectacle. That stuntman didn't know what hit him.

You know what you did, Evie Frye — you and your horrible brother. Now I'll fix you both. You know by now that I have Jacob, don't you? But you don't know where do you? You think you are smarter than me, Evie Frye? Well, you ain't, and neither is Jacob. He hangs now in a place where I hung him. He's alive, but he won't be for long. You can save him if you are smart enough to follow the clues. Find him by 10:48 tonight, or Jacob will die, and I will fix you too.

Bring none of your police friends. If the police come, he will die. If you come armed, then you will die — you both will die. I am

Through a daze, Selma realized that Jack had captured Josh! She realized that this deranged man actually thought Josh and she were Jacob and Evie Frye. The plans they had made were all wrong. They believed that Jack would go after Evie.

Thoughts ran rapidly through Selma's mind. How did Jack get Josh out of the building? Then she remembered the ambulance! An ambulance had almost run over the bum in town. There was an ambulance on the videos behind last year's Comic-Con. There was an ambulance in Orlando and Denver. He was using an ambulance to get his victims out of the crowd.

Selma raced at a dead run toward the loading dock. No ambulance. She quickly summoned the security guard. After flashing her badge, she questioned him about an ambulance.

"Sure did officer. He left just a few minutes ago," he grinned.

"Why was an ambulance here?"

"He said he had to pick up a resident. He was from a nursing home down south. It was from, uh…" the security guard scratched his head. "Oh, yeah! Gotham. It was Gotham Nursing Home. He loaded the guy up and drove away – probably about 15 minutes ago."

Selma went over everything she knew about the characters. She had to act quickly. What was the tie between the killer, Spring-heeled Jack, Jack the Ripper, and Batman? She went back to her room and changed her clothes. There was no way she was meeting this lunatic dressed as Evie Frye. She concealed her weapon and placed her phone on silent. She had to hurry. She knew that Jack intended to kill them both, but there was no reason to make it easier for him. Jack was not going to meet Evie Frye – he was going to meet Detective Selma Cibolo.

She flicked on her laptop and started researching Jack the Ripper and Spring-heeled Jack. There was a lot of information she already knew, but what had she missed? What had she forgotten? Spring-heeled Jack was thirty years before Jack the Ripper. She noted the similarity in names. It was clear in some of the games that there was a relationship between them. Selma recalled that in one game, they were father and son. In that scenario, Spring-heeled Jack, while a ghost, witnessed his son, Jack the Ripper's, assassination. Selma realized that Jack would have been powerless as a ghost.

She tried to figure out what Batman had to do with it. There were huge differences between Batman and the two Jacks. Batman did not appear on the scene until the 1930s. There was too much of a time between them. Batman did share some characteristics with both Spring-heeled and the Ripper. Selma also knew Batman never killed, which was more like Spring-heeled Jack than like Jack the Ripper. Something about Batman's family flashed in Selma's mind, so she typed it into the search engine.

Gotham City and Gotham Ambulance – there had to be a connection. Batman was Bruce Wayne, Selma knew. She read that a mugger had murdered his parents on the streets of Gotham City while they were returning from the cinema. Selma searched for Gotham Nursing home. She found a Gotham city on the laptop, but it was north near Dallas – not south. That must have been a diversion, she realized. Besides, Gotham near Dallas would be too far away. There wouldn't be time to drive there before 10:48 p.m.

What did the time have to do with anything? Why did Jack repeat that number – clue #1,048 and 10:48 on the clock? That could not be a coincidence. The killer did that so Selma would not miss the significance. But, what did it mean? Continuing to search, she found a Gotham Restaurant just outside Austin. It was close enough but too public to hold a hostage. It was the same story with the Gotham Club north of Austin.

Reading further down the page, Selma read an article that caught her attention. She was stunned to read that the mugger killed Batman's parents at 10:48 p.m. That was a clue! He was going to kill Josh at 10:48! There seemed to be something else about 1048. Still, nothing came to mind other than the similarity of the numbers and the time.

Selma recalled that Batman lived in a mansion in Gotham staffed by a butler named Alfred. A quick search showed Alfred, Texas, about 125 miles south of San Antonio. That was likely to be another false lead. Frustrated with the searching, she knew that Josh was in mortal danger, and here she was playing with her computer. She returned to the note.

Where else does Batman "hang" out, she wondered. Where do bats hang out? Batman has a bat cave, too – a bat cave! Of course! Selma had grown up around the area and immediately remembered the famous Bracken Bat Cave. The Bracken cave is home to the largest colony of Mexican free-tailed bats in the world. Selma had visited the cave dozens of times. She stood with dozens of bat fans at the rural cave entrance in the evenings to watch them fly out of a big hole in the ground. Several million bats would emerge each night between March and November, thrilling the naturalists and clouding radar screens in the region. The cave is in a protected area, but the caretakers open the viewing area during the season. It was the wrong time of the year; the bats had migrated to Mexico. In the offseason, the property is fenced off and locked. Is it possible, Jack could be holding Josh out there somewhere? The more she thought about it, the more she believed it was possible. Gathering her things, Selma rushed down the hall toward the elevator. She was convinced that somehow Jack was holding Josh in one of the outbuildings on the bat cave property. It would be a perfect hiding place. The bats had not migrated back in yet, and the property would be vacant. Selma remembered several ramshackle barns near the cave where earlier miners gathered guano to make gunpowder.

There was no time to wait. It was already getting dark. There was no time to call for backup. What if she were wrong? She couldn't afford another wild goose chase.

Hoping she was right, she drove her car north on IH-35 until she got to Natural Bridge Caverns Road. The bat cave was several miles to the west. Natural Bridge Caverns Road was also Texas Highway 46. Just before the caverns, Selma knew there was an unmarked entrance to the bat cave property. Highway 46 was a two-lane blacktopped road that wound through the edge of the hill country. The sun had gone, and the lack of light concealed some of the features along the route. Trees and buildings formed silhouettes against a red Texas sunset. She hoped she could remember where the unmarked entrance was. Fifteen miles down the road, just before the highway made a sweeping curve to the north at the Caverns and Exotic Game Ranch, Selma pulled her car over on the left shoulder of the road. It was almost fully dark now, but the hidden sun feathered clouds with a silver lining. It was as if someone had taken a white marker and outlined them. Lightning from the earlier rainstorm still flashed on the northern horizon. She pulled a flashlight from her glove compartment and walked a short way down the grassy area to a gate in the rusty barbed wire fence.

She looked down the winding dirt road that led to the cave. It did not appear that anyone had been in there lately. The wet grass still stood high and not bent down by passing car wheels, and no tracks passed through the gate. A heavy steel padlock was still locked, and a spider web stretched from the lock to the nearest post. Selma's heart sank as she realized no one had been through this gate in several weeks. Was there another way to the cave? Aware that Jack might be watching, Selma leaned close to her car's floorboard and opened the map feature on her phone. It did not appear that there were any other entrances to the bat cave property.

Just as she turned off the phone, Selma remembered something she had seen before on this road. Turning the GPS back on, she enlarged the map and found what she was looking for – Bat Cave Road, about six miles back toward the east on Highway 46. In the gathering darkness, she had missed it.

Jamming her car in gear, she made a wide U-turn and headed back the way she came. Pulling to the side of the road once more, she noted that on the north was Bat Cave Loop, and on up the road on the other side a ways, was Bat Cave Road. It was an odd name for a road unless it linked up to a bat cave. Is there an unmarked and forgotten entrance to the bat cave from that road? Why would someone name it Bat Cave Road if it did not go to the bat cave? "One way to find out," she muttered to herself. She did not want to go on a loop, so she turned south down a dark rural Bat Cave Road.

The few houses on the road were spaced far apart. Open fields divided the mostly ancient and ramshackle farmhouses. The farms looked like spooky Halloween houses with the moon shining through heavy clouds and lightning flashing here and there. The farmland lay fallow this time of the year, but she could see the farmers still planted hay and field corn in season. Between the houses, round bales of hay, and rusting farm equipment sat silent witness. Most of the lights Selma saw were automatic halogen security lights that hung from barns and outbuildings. Selma slowly guided her car from house to house, looking for an old road or even a path that might lead toward the bat cave. A rumble of thunder announced that another storm was closing in quickly. Selma smelled rain mixed with dirt in the air.

Signs along the fence line advertised eggs and hay for sale – baled or rounds. Across an old barbed wire fence, three black cows chewed their cuds and watched Selma intently. They mooed at her, probably expecting Selma to feed them. An old battered sign with peeling paint informed passersby that the Stanton Rabbit Ranch was just ahead. At the gate to the rabbit ranch, the grass lay flattened in the ditch. Muddy tire tracks led in toward a barn-like building in the back. It looked abandoned, but it was clear that someone had been there recently. There was no security light, but a single yellow bulb flickered inside an outbuilding. At least the place still had electricity.

As Selma stopped at a string of mailboxes along the fence, the one near the gate caught her attention. A flash of lightning caught the letters on the old tilted mailbox. The letters STANTON in flaking white paint stood out against the dull rusting metal mailbox on Bat Cave Road. Beneath the faded name were the numbers: 1048.

# 28

Selma drove her car about a quarter-mile from the Stanton ranch. Jack would probably be watching the road, she thought. She pulled over where the road made a little curve to the south. A small grove of shrub trees grew along the side of the road would block anyone watching from the house. She parked her car and got out, looking at the sky. It wasn't raining yet, but it could start at any moment. A jagged streak of lightning flashed just before a big boomer filled her ears. That was close. Not wanting to be the tallest thing on the road, she moved across the bar ditch and moved along the trees and stumpy bushes along the fence line. She was careful not to touch the barbed wire fence.

Across a field, she could see the house was set back off the road a short distance. There wasn't much cover between the road and the gate. Anyone could easily spot her walking up the muddy lane that led to the house. "Stanton Rabbit Ranch" and "No Trespassing" signs were wired along the fence. The east side of the house had few windows, so Selma decided her best approach would be to cross the wire and come in from the side. She would be unseen unless someone were watching from those windows. She figured if Jack were waiting for her, he would be watching the driveway, not the open field alongside.

Getting across the fence was not a problem, except she snagged the cuff of her pants on the barbs. She jerked it free and slogged her way through the stubble of an old hayfield. She was glad she had worn good shoes but wished she had kept on Evie's boots. With every step, water and mud slopped over the sides of her shoe and ran inside. She loved the sweet smell of mown hay that surrounded her. The grass had a heavenly aroma that you could barely smell from the road, but the scent was heady as you walked through it. By the time she reached the fence that ran next to the house, her feet were soaked and cold.

She was confident but not completely sure no one had seen her. She climbed between the barbed wires of the fence. Preferring to be as safe as possible, she placed her ear to the cold, wet house siding and listened. No sound or light came from inside the house. Hugging as close to the wall as possible, Selma peered around the corner toward the front. Nothing moved in the vacant field in front of the house. There was no car, just muddy tracks that led down the drive. Someone was here.

Lightning flashed, and she felt little sprinkles as she turned and worked her way along the side of the house, ducking beneath the few windows. At the corner of the house, she saw an old barn with a soft yellow light visible through the cracks and openings. Selma noted another outbuilding near the barn, which appeared to be a garage. Muddy tire tracks ended at the large overhead door. She realized a car was in there behind that door. Several small pens on stilt legs lined the back of the house, and a rock path led to the barn. Chicken wire covered the little cages. Selma noted the bottom of the nearest cage held moldy rabbit feed as she slipped around the corner into the backyard. Probably remnants of their last meal, she thought cynically.

Selma realized she had to clear that garage before things went any further. Jack could be hiding in there, waiting for her to head directly to the barn. Realizing she would be in the open unprotected, she circled behind the dilapidated garage. One more mix-up like San Francisco with the police arresting an innocent, retired rabbit farmer would probably end her career. She had to check out that car before she got in any deeper. Looking at her watch, she saw it was past nine o'clock. She still had time before 10:48.

Only a pump house and a rusty butane tank stood between the house and the rundown garage. They would be the only cover she would have. Stooping low, she ran for the pump house. The pump shed was a short wooden silo that barely covered the equipment inside. She was afraid if she leaned on it too much, it might topple over. The paint was peeling from the rough wooden sides. Selma shivered as a north wind picked up and fluttered down her shirt. Not good, she thought. It's about to rain a frog strangler. She wondered why she thought of that old euphemism for a storm. She had not used it in years. Her father used to say that – frog strangler. Selma hoped she wouldn't be the frog.

The storm was coming fast, so she decided it would be best to be under some kind of roof when it happened – even if the ceiling were falling around her head. Taking a deep breath, she sprinted toward the garage. In her haste, she pulled against the door handle before realizing someone had locked the door with a padlock. It was a dumb mistake. She hoped she hadn't made too much noise. Circling to the rear of the building, she found an opening that once held a window case. It was now just an open hole in the wall. Peering in, she could see nothing in the dark. She realized that no one could put a padlock on a door from the inside. Hitching herself up, she pulled herself through the window just as fat, wet drops of rain began to splatter against the side of the building.

Selma stood still for a few moments listening for any movement. There was none, so she fished in her pockets for her flashlight. Shielding the lens with her palm to avoid a harsh glare of light, she turned it on. Lifting her palm carefully to emit only enough light for her to see, Selma found herself standing in front of a white truck. Her heart skipped a beat in her chest as she realized it was a van – a white van. Moving along the side, Selma saw the wheelchair lift. In the rear, she noted the Texas plates. She traced the raised numbers on the license plate and knew this was it! It was the same van she had seen in the Orlando parking lot. It had to be. Raising her light a little further, she illuminated the magnetic sign that read Gotham City Ambulance.

Selma sighed with relief as she realized she had found Jack at last. But, where was he? Where was Josh? They had to be somewhere close by – probably in that huge barn. Selma decided to clear the van before she went any further. Jack was probably not inside, given the padlock on the door, but maybe Josh was. Dousing the light, Selma quietly eased the side door open. The interior light did not come on. Carefully she squeezed inside the dark van. Something immediately grabbed Selma by the neck. A rough strap wrapped around her head and forced her against the door. Gasping in horror, she realized it was only the seatbelt. Flicking on her flashlight again, she verified that the van was empty.

She didn't dare close the door, fearing the sound would be heard outside. He knew she was here anyway, she thought. Hoping that Jack would think it would take her more time to locate his hideout, she went back through the open window hole to the outside. Jack was probably still watching the road – more than likely from that barn. She hoped he would not expect anyone to come up from the rear.

Selma was grateful that the rain had slowed to a fine mist. Maybe it wouldn't be a frog strangler after all. The bulk of the storm looped around to the east of IH-35 like most of them do. From behind the garage, Selma studied the barn. It was in poor condition compared to the rest of the buildings. In addition to the peeling paint, half of the roof had caved in at one corner. Since there were no windows in the barn, Selma slowly crept to toward the building. She pressed her ear to the wall. Each rumble of thunder caused the entire building to shake; each flash of lightning revealed a horrific scene. There was no sound except the building creaking in the wind. Carefully peering around the corner of the barn, Selma saw a large sliding main door. It was partly open. Hearing nothing, Selma crept along the wall to the doorway.

Selma reviewed the story from here. Jack, in his deluded mind, believed himself to be the reincarnation of Spring-heeled Jack. He wanted revenge on Evie and Jacob for killing his son, Jack the Ripper. Jack intended to kill both her and Josh, thinking they were the real assassins. All of the girls Jack had killed were dressed as Evie Frye. Selma hoped that when Jack saw her dressed as Selma, it would break the spell, and he would realize that Selma was not Evie Frye. It was a big risk. If he did not, Selma realized she would have to kill Jack herself. Selma pulled her gun and eased toward the open door, determined, come what may, to find out what was inside.

The door was not quite open wide enough for Selma to slip through. She would need both hands to pull the door wider. Placing her gun back in its holster, she leaned her body against the heavy door and slid it back a few inches more. Selma cringed as it made a rumbling noise as it slid on its rails.

For the second time this night, Selma's neck was caught in a tight grip. Before she could grab her weapon, rough hands dragged her into the darkness of the barn. Struggling weakly against her attacker, Selma looked up into the face of Spring-heeled Jack as a flash of lightning lit the barn as bright as day! Jack quickly overpowered Selma as he carried her by the neck toward a large table in the middle of the room. The room plunged back into utter darkness as the lightning faded. In horror, Selma realized it was the table where rabbits were butchered. Jack flung her onto the table. She lay stunned and terrified, trying to catch her breath. Jack swiftly tied her arms and legs to ropes attached to the table. Clutching her throat again, he took her to the point of oblivion before he eased the pressure. Jack knew how to keep his victims conscious yet helpless on the edge of the void. A soft glow came from a single bulb swinging from a wire from the ceiling. When her eyes adjusted to the dim light again, Selma could see Josh suspended above her. He was in some type of sling, hung from the ceiling by chains. Dozens of large hooks hung from the rafters. Laughing insanely, Jack forced Selma's mouth open and stuffed a rag down her throat. Overpowered and gagging, Selma realized it was useless to resist. She stopped struggling to conserve her strength. She waited for an opportunity to fight back.

Selma realized that Josh was aware, but he too was gagged, so he could not speak. He was held aloft, his arms and legs locked in a spread-eagle position. Jack circled the table, tightening Selma's ropes, his maniacal laughter filling the barn. Satisfied that Selma was tightly secured to the table, Jack stepped back to admire his work. Selma thought it was like a scene from some bizarre melodrama. The laughter is pure Joker-like.

Jack looked up toward Josh. "Ah, Jacob, my dear, behold your precious sister. All trussed up, ready for the slaughter. Look how quietly, powerlessly, she lies before her master. You will have to watch. You have no other choice unless you close your eyes. You will see how easily she slips under my power. How she hungrily accepts her fate. What? Can't you see her well enough? Let me fix that problem for you, dear Jacob. I wouldn't want you to miss anything."

Grasping the loose chains that hung from Josh's restraints, Jack ratcheted Josh downward even closer to the table. The image of Selma came more clearly into view. Josh can see Selma stretched on the table, arms above her head and immobilized. Jack had tied her legs to the bottom of the table, leaving her legs spread in an obscene position. Slowly lowered, Josh realized he could now reach his gun. Just a few more inches, he begs silently – only one more cog on that gear.

At the click of the cogwheel, Josh grabbed his gun and pointed it directly at Jack. Instead of shrinking back in fear, Jack laughed. Josh pulled the trigger as the gun merely clicked on an empty chamber. Jack clutched his chest, pretending to be shot, and fell to his knees.

Jack staggered to his feet wildly laughing. "You sap! How did you ever become a cop?"

Josh pulled the trigger three more times in his frustration, knowing the gun had been emptied. Jack moved toward Josh and presented his chest to Josh as close as possible, laughing all the while. Josh tried to throw the gun at Jack, but the firearm tumbled harmlessly to the floor.

"What now?" Jack sneered. "No one is coming to rescue you – no one knows where you are. This property has been abandoned for twenty years. So, if you are finished with the theatrics, you can watch what I do to her. Later, you'll get your turn." The insane laughter filled the barn.

Jack slowly pulled a large butcher knife and rubbed his thumb across the blade. He slowly sucked blood from his thumb as he looked deeply into Josh's eyes. He moved so near his face Josh feared Jack was about to kiss him. Jack turned slowly toward Selma with a cruel grin and began to cut off her clothing. Selma's terrified eyes fixed on Josh's as they both realized that they were stuck – no one was coming to help them. Batman was nowhere around.

# 29

Slowly and methodically, Jack began to cut off Selma's clothing. Selma lay in terror as, one by one, Jack snipped the buttons from her shirt, revealing her slip. Jack frequently paused to admire his work. He worked slowly, knowing he had all the time in the world. The thought came to Selma that he was preparing her like a butcher would prepare meat. Lying on the rough cutting board, Selma realized exactly what Jack intended to do.

With no hope and no other options, Selma struggled and twisted, trying to disrupt his process. It was no use. She was tightly bound to the cutting board and completely helpless. Her protestations only brought on more insane laughter from Jack.

Jack checked his watch. "Almost time, my dear," he said with a grisly grin. "Go ahead and scream," he taunted. "No one is going to hear you except Jacob, and he's in no position to help!" Turning to Jacob, Jack goaded, "How is your position, Jacob?"

Turning back to Selma, Jack pulled the choking cloth from her mouth. She retched as the rag was withdrawn from her throat. "We don't need this, my dear Evie. Do we? We don't need to cover that kissable mouth."

Freed from the gag, Selma twisted her head to avoid his repulsive lips. She tried to reason with Jack as much as she could. "Listen. You've made a big mistake. I'm not who you think I am. I'm not Evie Frye, and he's not Jacob. He's a police officer from Denver named Josh Logan, and I'm with the San Antonio police department. My name is Selma Cibolo. We aren't who you think we are. We are here to help you. Can't you understand? You've become obsessed with a game. Nothing bad will happen to you if you release us. We know it was a big mistake. Let us help you."

Jack waved the dirty cloth in front of her face. "You want me to put this back in? I liked it better when you were scared. Now shut up!"

Selma's heart leaped in her chest. A flash of lightning revealed how hopeless her situation was. Josh was in no position to help her. No one knew where she was. Selma realized how far out on a limb she had placed them by not sharing her information and location with Thorn. Now she would pay the price. There was no one to help her.

Jack turned to Josh, "Can you see how she is? Your sister just can't keep her mouth shut." Turning back to Selma, he lowered his face close to hers. "What am I going to do with you?"

"I … I don't know," Selma stuttered, knowing full well what he intended. She squirmed as he continued to peel her clothing away as if he were skinning a rabbit. He stood and circled the table, admiring his work. He adjusted the straps that confined her to the rough board. Satisfied that Selma was in the proper position, he turned to taunt Josh again.

"Almost time. You can watch what I do before she dies," Jack said. "At least when I do it, it's not incest. You've been a bad boy, Jacob. A very bad boy. It's time you both pay for your betrayal." Jack laughed and turned back to Selma.

In one smooth motion, he pounced back on the table and knelt between Selma's outstretched legs. "It's time," he breathed into Selma's face. Selma struggled and wrenched away from the weight of Jack's body. She felt hands clasp around her throat. As her airway was compressed, Selma felt the weight of his torso shift. It was like her body was being suffocated and constricted at the same time. Selma wanted him off. She bucked and twisted, but he was too heavy. Tightening his grip around her neck, Jack was slowly squeezing the life from her. Bright flashes and hallucinations began to spark in Selma's brain. In a brief moment of lightning, Selma saw a crowd of comic superheroes circled at the end of the table. Were they real? Were they really there? In the dim light, they looked alive. She tried to focus as the pressure on her throat became almost unbearable. Batman was there, fully dressed, as was Spring-heeled Jack. One of them looked strangely like Jack the Ripper. One statue was completely nude, with his sexless body standing at an odd angle.

Deep in her mind, Selma remembered the police report from Arizona that the suspect had an assortment of manikins in his car. As she fell deeper into the black of semi-consciousness, Selma realized that these were the same body models that spooked the cop in Arizona. What deluded purpose did they serve? Why had Jack taken the time to set them up on their little stands and dress them in costumes? It was too odd to be believable.

Outside, the storm regained its fury as the rain began in earnest. Heavy raindrops beat against the roof of the old barn. Terrified, Selma hoped it would blow the barn down around them. Maybe if the roof fell in on them, Jack might die in the wreckage. Selma realized she was grasping at straws. A collapsed building would kill her and Josh as well. What escape was that? The only satisfaction would be that Jack would not get his – what? Satisfaction? Passion? Revenge?

Selma heard Jack talking to Josh again as though through a thick fog. "Watch as she dies," he mocked. "You are fully impotent to help her. She is going to die right in front of you, and there isn't a thing you can do," Jack laughed.

The room began to grow even gloomier than it was. Was that lightning? Bright flashes of light came again and again as Selma struggled to breathe. Selma was starving for air. In her mind, she rose from the table and floated above the scene. She could see herself under the great weight of the fiend that was choking the life out of her. Lightning illuminated the scene below her as the manikins cast weird shadows against the rough walls of the old barn. Other sparks and flashes of colored light began to streak around the room. It was not lightning, she thought. What was the word to describe those weird flashes? She knew what it was – phosphene. That's it! Phosphene lights!

Just seconds before she faded to black, Jack released the pressure on her neck enough for her to breathe. As her lungs filled, Selma's body jerked as oxygen brought relief to tortured organs. She felt her head clear as she became more aware. She was no longer floating above the room. The enormous weight of him continued to press down on her. Jack knew exactly what he was doing.

Knowing the life was being slowly squeezed out of her, Selma made one last desperate attempt to escape. She heaved her body upwards as hard as she could, trying to push Jack off balance. With her legs and arms tied to the corners of the table, she could only use her torso. It was not good. Jack only laughed again in that demented way that brought chills down her spine.

Slowly Jack's hand tightened again, and she felt herself floating down a long dark tunnel toward unconsciousness with only the phosphene lights to guide her way. She lifted her head to see the doorway and freedom. The door seemed so far away. Selma realized she was going to die on this table. Just before she passed out, a clash of thunder filled her ears, and a long streak of light stretched out from the darkness.

There was another flash of lightning followed by more thunder as it began to rain. Rain fell on Selma's cheeks and bare shoulders. The pressure on her throat eased. Half stunned by the lack of air Selma gulped the life-giving air into her lungs. Something in Selma's mind realized the flashes she saw were neither lightning nor phosphene. That sound she heard was not thunder. She recognized a muzzle blast. Looking up over the top of her head toward the darkened doorway, she saw the weapon explode again.

More rain fell on Selma's face as the enormous weight slid from her body onto the floor. Jack's heavy body slid to the floor like a dead deer carcass. Quickly moving her head, she arched her neck upward as far as she could to see the doorway more clearly. A figure holding a smoking gun emerged from the shadows of the entrance. Before everything faded to black, Selma saw someone emerge from the darkened doorway. Quasimodo.

# 30

Thorn stepped from the doorway and pulled his hood back. He moved quickly to Selma's motionless body. Uniformed police SWAT team officers pushed past him as they secured Jack's lifeless body. Other police were busy freeing Josh from his harness. Another officer collected Jack's knife and tied it in a plastic bag. Emergency response teams followed with a gurney that carried neatly stacked blankets and medical equipment. Thorn grabbed a blue medical blanket, shook it out, and covered Selma. Light began to fill the room as work lights were set up at the crime scene.

"Sir," one of the EMTs protested, "we have to examine her."

Thorn fixed him with a cold stare. "Examine her, then!" Thorn barked. "I'm staying right here with her. Work around me," he ordered.

Selma slowly became aware of what was happening to her. As she returned to consciousness, she felt tight pressure on her right hand. Glancing down, Selma saw her hand disappear into a meaty fist. She followed the hairy arm upwards to find Thorn's stony face. She became vaguely aware that his other palm caressed her forehead as he brushed her hair aside. Thorn? Had Thorn been Quasimodo at those other shows? Had he been following her?

"What the hell is that?" Thorn asked, indicating the half dozen manikins arranged around the foot of the table.

"We don't know, sir," a medic responded. "Those are dummies. We don't know what they're for."

"Witnesses," Selma rasped, her throat raw and sore. "They were witnesses."

Thorn's face contorted in disgust. "What? Witnesses? That was one sick puppy!"

The medics checked her airway and took her pulse and temperature. Under Thorn's watchful eye, they pulled back the blanket to examine her for other injuries. Not finding any, the first responders began to wash her chest and face.

Selma became aware that they were not washing away raindrops. They were cleaning Jack's blood from her face and torso. Selma looked up into Thorn's concerned eyes. She had not noticed before how kind his eyes were. Now they looked at her differently. Selma felt safe with him there.

Josh had been lowered and was standing on his feet as other medics examined him for injuries.

The medics began to ask Selma questions about her name, where she was, and what day she thought it was. She kept her eyes on Thorn as she answered. Her head cleared slowly as every part of her body ached. She felt sore and exhausted.

"Sir, we have to move her," Selma heard an attendant say. "You have to let her go."

Thorn's gruff voice responded, "No."

"Sir, we have to move her to the gurney," the medic insisted. "We have to get her in the ambulance. She's **our** patient," the young man asserted.

Thorn gave the young aide a look that stopped him in his tracks. "She's **my** partner," Thorn grunted as he gathered Selma in his arms. "I'll take her." Thorn carefully moved Selma to the gurney. He laid her gently on the rolling stretcher and took her hand again. "I'm going with her," he advised the medical team in a way that left no question in their minds.

As they rolled Selma across the bumpy dirt driveway and lifted her cart into the ambulance, Thorn never left her side.

She rapidly grew stronger and more conscious. Selma's voice was raspy and weak. Her tongue felt thick and heavy. "We got him?" she croaked.

"We got him," Thorn assured her as the litter was lifted into the ambulance.

"Who was he?" Selma asked as the rear doors slammed shut. "Why did he do all this?"

As the ambulance bumped down the driveway onto the street, Thorn filled her in. "His name was Jack Kupp," he told her.

"Jack? His name really was Jack?"

"Yeah," Thorn admitted. "He was a piece of work. He worked in the movie prop business setting up scenes for horror movies – or at least he did until the last year or so. The film crews refused to work with him, claiming he was too disruptive – and too weird." Thorn chuckled, "That's saying something for that crowd."

"He had a place in San Diego and several other ones around the country where Comic-Cons were held. The FBI is checking all those places out for evidence. They've already tied him to several murders in various places."

"Orlando," Selma's voice scratched.

"And, other places, including San Antonio," Thorn assured her. "He's your killer, Selma. Anyway," Thorn continued, "working in the movies, he had access to various accounts, names, and identities he could use. It was pretty easy to check on these different forged IDs. He was off the grid," Thorn nodded. "He paid cash everywhere he went. He didn't stay in motels. He didn't leave any trail that might come back to him. We'd have never found him if not for you," Thorn assured her.

Tears welled in Selma's eyes as Thorn continued, "Fired from his movie gig, he hid out in his house and played video games constantly. He got so engrossed; he forgot who he was. He became a character in the game – a character that hated your character."

"Spring-heeled Jack," Selma's voice scraped.

"Yeah, he imagined he was that guy. He got to where he couldn't tell real life from a game. In his mind, he became the person – just like you said. He had this strange idea your character had done him wrong somehow – this, who was it? Sadie?"

"Evie Frye," Selma offered. "He imagined she killed his father."

"Yeah! Her! Anyway, he stalked her at every convention. He would somehow lure the girls out of the building and abduct them. Sometimes he'd tell them they were shooting a movie. Sometimes he'd pose as an ambulance driver, telling the girls that their mother had been in an auto accident. It was more of him living out his fantasy delusion than a sex thing, although he did molest and kill most of them."

"How?" Selma asked.

"Oh, the usual way, I guess. Suffocation. You know he had a signature pattern like most killers do. It was like he was exacting revenge, and I guess, in his mind, he was."

"No," Selma coughed. "I mean, how did you find out where we were? How did you find us?"

"Oh, that," Thorn smiled. "Simple. Good police work. We checked new Texas plates issued in the last three months. It took some doing, but the State finally coughed them up. We found a tag registered to a white van with a wheelchair lift out in Marfa. It was strange because the guy did not want a handicapped placard. Who needs a wheelchair lift without a blue hanger? So, we followed up on that. He wasn't at the address he used, and he had not been there for over a month. Paid a year in advance, too -- in cash, of course. We talked to the vehicle registrar in Marfa and found out the van had been previously registered in California – guess where? San Diego! We staked out the place in Marfa, but he never showed back up. We followed you out to San Francisco, but we didn't spot him. So, we thought he might show up here in San Antonio."

"You knew?" Selma gasped.

"We knew. We started looking for that van. We never found it. He never got on the freeway – kept to the backroads and such."

"So, how did you find him then?"

"We didn't," Thorn grinned. "We found you. We put a tail on you, but you lost him tonight up by the caverns. They didn't expect you to do a U-turn. So, they had to call another unmarked car in. By the time he showed up, you weren't on the road anymore. So they circled the area and finally picked you up. The unit showed up just in time to see you being pulled inside the barn. They called the swat team and me. I got here before they did – and just in time too, looks like!"

How did you find the place? The van was out of sight."

"Come on," Thorn laughed. "Give me some props – that's how you say it. Props?"

Selma laughed, though it hurt her ribs. "Yeah, ten years ago."

"Yeah! A batman in a bat cave, on a bat road? Good police work, that's all. I knew what you were up to – I've been tailing you for two weeks."

Selma remembered San Francisco. "As Quasimodo?" She laughed.

Thorn acted offended. "Come on! "It's the only costume that fit," he admitted. Show a little gratitude, will ya'?"

Selma squeezed Thorn's hand a little tighter. "Thank you, Thorn," she croaked.

"After all," Thorn reminded her, "I chased Batman down a rabbit hole for you."

# 31

Everyone in the hallway at headquarters stopped to congratulate Selma as she worked her way to her office. The office was empty as Selma flipped on the light switch. She cringed as she looked at the overflowing in-basket. Cases were piling up since Thorn had been following her. Now he had been placed on administrative leave after the shooting. Any time an officer discharged his weapon, there had to be an inquiry.

Meanwhile, crime did not take a break. Selma saw long hours ahead, catching up with the backlog. Selma realized she needed coffee before she dove into this morass of files and records.

In the break room, a group crowded around the television. Selma silently moved in behind them. Selma recognized the scene on the television immediately. She shuddered as though some invisible force drew her into that place again. She wanted to shout to the reporter not to go into that barn. The reporter, dressed in a raincoat, held an umbrella in one hand and a microphone in the other, talked to the camera.

"Barbara, I'm standing in front of this dilapidated barn out on the far northeast side of Bexar County. It was here in this old barn where two police officers were held hostage last night. Somehow, a suspect wanted for questioning in a series of murders overpowered and held them hostage. In a dramatic rescue, Detective Sergeant Thorn Nix freed his partner, Detective Selma Cibolo, from her abductor. Detective Nix could not speak with us in person, but we managed to catch up to him on the phone.

Unwilling to provide us with names or details, Detective Nix informed us that the two detectives had been trailing this suspect for several weeks. They finally cornered the suspect in this abandoned rabbit farm out on Bat Cave Road. Thorn said he arrived on the scene just in time to save the lives of both detectives. The suspect was killed in the rescue. His name has not been released, pending further investigation. As you can see behind me, officers are still processing the crime scene."

"Wow, Maria! That sounds like a scene out of a horror movie."

"It must have seemed that way to them, too, Barbara. Although Detective Nix did not identify the suspect, he told us that the man was involved in a series of multiple killings and abductions at comic conventions around the country. One of the detectives was out of Denver and had also searched for this suspect for some time. Detective Nix credits his partner Detective Cibolo for solving the crime and tracking down the assailant. Nix was adamant that without Cibolo's expert investigation, they may never have caught this elusive attacker. Detective Nix is on administrative leave pending an investigation into this matter. We'll bring you more on this exciting story as we get it. From Bat Cave Road, this is Maria Galvan for KBX-TV news."

Selma jumped and caught her breath as someone tapped her on the shoulder.

"I'm sorry," the police officer apologized. "I shouldn't have come up behind you like that."

"It's okay," Selma assured him as she caught her breath. It would be a while before her nerves settled down, she thought. "Don't worry about it," she said, smiling. "I'm still a little jumpy, I guess."

"Don't blame you," the officer agreed. "We went through the academy together, remember me?" He asked.

"Yes," Selma nodded. "Pete, isn't it? Peter …" Selma read from his name tag: "Peter Hoskins. I do remember you – it's been a long time."

"Yes. That's right. Two years. You've really moved up in the department. We're all proud of you. That was some deal last night. I'm glad you made it out."

"Yeah," Selma agreed. "Me too."

"They sent me down here to find you," Peter continued. "The Chief wants you up in his office right away. They've got the Captain up there too, so I guess it's about last night. They didn't seem real happy, just so you know."

"Thank you, Pete. I'll head on up there then."

Well, this can't be good, Selma thought as she rode the elevator up to the top floor executive suites. Time to pay the fiddler. She hadn't spoken to Thorn since the EMTs wheeled her into the emergency room the night before. By the time they released her, Thorn had left. She rode a taxi home. Now he's on administrative leave, and she has to face this inquiry alone.

Now, what? She wondered as she entered the Chief's outer office. "They're waiting for you, dear," the assistant said as she led Selma to the Chief's conference room. She patted Selma on the shoulder as she said, "You know you're my new hero, don't you?"

"Thanks," Selma smiled. A new hero without a job, she thought to herself. This was going to be hard. She swallowed the lump in her throat and stepped into the room. The Chief sat at the head of the table. Thorn sat on the side with his hat in his hands dangling between his legs. She was happy to see him. Capt. Rangell sat next to Thorn. Both wore worried looks. On the other side of the table sat two officers she didn't know. From the way they were dressed, Selma sensed they were law enforcement. They wore cowboy boots, crisp white shirts, and ties. The crisp white shirts looked spotless, like they had just come from the cleaners. They were probably internal affairs, Selma guessed as she looked around the room. Two Stetsons hung from the hat rack by the door. Uh oh, she thought, looking back at the two strangers. Texas Rangers! She was in big trouble!

"Sit down, Cibolo," the Chief pointed to an empty chair. Selma could not tell from the inflection of his voice whether it was an order or an invitation. She sat and smiled at the men in the room, not knowing what was coming next but fearing the worst. Falling back on her training, Selma decided to say nothing unless she was asked a direct question. This scene had bad trouble written all over it.

The Chief spoke first. "Cibolo, you know the Captain and Sergeant Nix. These two men are U.S. Marshals Timmons and Ivy." Selma's heart sank. U.S. Marshals! It was worse than she feared – we're talking federal here. She tried to maintain her poker face.

The two Marshals rose to shake her hand and sat back down. Selma took a deep breath and turned to face them as the Chief continued. "Cibolo, you're pretty new on the force. Please tell these men a little about you and your career so far."

Selma told them about the academy and that she had been on the force a little over three years. She said she was assigned to the Homicide Division and worked under Sergeant Nix. Not knowing what else they wanted, she stopped talking, waiting for a clue about what she should say next. She clasped her hands together in her lap to keep them from shaking.

Marshal Timmons asked calmly, "Three years, and you are already a detective?"

Before she could respond, the Chief piped in, "Timmons, you wouldn't believe it! This girl pert-near aced that test in her second year on the force! No one has ever done that in my recollection."

"So, we heard," Timmons nodded. "That's pretty impressive. What tuned you into this guy – this Jack Kupp fellow? What made you suspect he was committing these abductions around the country?"

"I didn't know it was him – or who he was. I just found out that the same female character was being abducted and killed at Comic-Cons around the country. We had one abducted here last year and one killed a year before that."

"And this character was, who?" Timmons asked.

"Her name is Evie Frye. Those who go to Comic-Cons often dress up as a character from a game or a story. Evie is a fictional character who appears in the game Assassin's Revenge."

"So, you deduced from this game a list of characters who might have it in for Evie Frye?" Timmons asked.

"Yes, sir," Selma admitted.

The two Marshals looked at each other and nodded. "And, what did you come up with?" Timmons continued.

"We thought that the actual killer might be posing as a character named Spring-heeled Jack."

"How did you come to that conclusion?"

"Legend has it that Spring-heeled Jack was the father of Jack the Ripper. There are a lot of similarities between them: they work in the dark of night, they can leap incredible distances, they wear black costumes, and they have unusual superpowers. Spring-heeled Jack was active a decade or so before Jack the Ripper and was reported in several London newspapers. Although Spring-heeled Jack didn't kill anyone, as far as anyone knows, he did attack young women in the middle of the night and frightened them almost to death. No one ever caught either Jack, so the legend has existed since Victorian times. They were the prototype for several of the comic super-heroes in comics and movies today – Batman, Superman, The Lantern, and several others."

"Okay. Why did you think Jack would kill this time? What did this Spring-heeled Jack have against Evie Frye?" Timmons wanted to know.

Selma took a deep breath; this wasn't turning out so bad after all, she thought. "Well, again, according to legend and the history of the game itself – which is mostly fiction – Evie and her brother Jacob were assassins."

"Assassins?" Timmons seemed confused. "I thought they were the good guys."

"Well," Selma laughed, "they are 'good' assassins. They only kill the bad guys – like Jack the Ripper. Which is why Spring-heeled Jack had it in for Evie Frye – she killed his son."

"Ah, I see," Timmons nodded. "So, you needed to find out who was showing up at Comic-Con dressed a Spring-heeled Jack?"

"Yes, sir. But it wasn't that easy. It turned out that Kupp had several disguises and identities."

"So, you got the bright idea of dressing up like Evie Frye and luring him out of hiding?" Timmons said accusingly.

Playtime was over. Now it was going to get rough. "Yes, sir," Selma admitted.

Timmons sat back and pressed his hands together in front of his face before he spoke. He rested his chin on his thumbs as he considered his next question. Selma squirmed uncomfortably in her chair. Here it comes, she thought. My career is over.

Marshal Timmons dropped his hands and looked at his partner as he began to speak. "This is amazing." Ivey shrugged his shoulders. Timmons turned back to Selma, "I don't know how many rules, regulations, or laws you've broken, Detective Cibolo." He began to tick them off on the fingers of his hand. "You went outside your chain of command. You exceeded your authority. You went out of your jurisdiction as you raced around the country. You got an innocent man's home raided by the FBI. You got another detective from Denver suspended. You risked his life and your own by getting abducted by the suspect you were tracking. You're lucky you both weren't murdered. You got your Sergeant placed on administrative leave for killing a suspect to save your life. National news media is going nuts over this, and we can't squash the story. What do you have to say for yourself?"

Selma looked toward the Chief. "Am I fired?" She asked.

Marshal Timmons placed both hands on his head, brushed his hair back, and looked at the ceiling. "Fired?" He barked. Fixing Selma with a piercing stare, he shook his head. "Detective Cibolo," he paused a moment before he continued, "we're here to recruit you for the U. S. Marshal's Service."

■■■■■■■■■■■■■■■■■■■■■■■■■■■■■■■■■■■■■■■■■■■■■■■■■■■

A week later, Selma had cleaned out her office and packed her bags. She was headed for 21-weeks at the Marshals Training Academy in Glencoe, Georgia. After a heartfelt goodbye, Thorn and Rangell watched her leave from the large window in Rangell's office.

"Our little girl has grown up and left us," Rangell teased.

"Don't start, George. I'm not in the mood."

"Lighten up, buttercup. You didn't want her anyway. You stood right here in this office and swore you didn't want her! Begged me to give her to someone else. Remember that?"

"I was wrong," Thorn admitted. "Go ahead and rub it in."

"Well," Rangell drawled, "maybe you'll get a new one."

Thorn watched Selma drive out of the police parking area. "Nah," he shook his head, "they don't make 'em like that anymore."

Rangell laughed out loud. "What are you talkin' about? She's twenty-five years old for cryin' out loud!" Rangell handed Thorn a neatly wrapped package. "Here, Bunny sent you something. She thought it would put you in a better mood. Don't open it until you get back to your desk."

Back at his desk, Thorn could not help but laugh as he unwrapped a yellow pencil cup with a smiley face on the side.

The End.